melville house classics

THE ART OF THE NOVELLA

THE GIRL WITH THE GOLDEN EYES

THE GIRL WITH THE GOLDEN EYES

HONORÉ DE BALZAC

Boca Raton Public Library, Boca Raton, FL

MELVILLE HOUSE PUBLISHING
HOBOKEN, NEW JERSEY

FIRST PUBLISHED IN 1835 IN THE COLLECTION,
HISTORY OF THE THIRTEEN.

BOOK DESIGN: DAVID KONOPKA

MELVILLE HOUSE PUBLISHING
300 OBSERVER HIGHWAY
THIRD FLOOR
HOBOKEN, NJ 07030

WWW.MHPBOOKS.COM

FIRST MELVILLE HOUSE PRINTING: DECEMBER 2007
ISBN: 978-0-9766583-1-3
PRINTED IN CANADA

LIBRARY OF CONGRESS CATALOGING-IN-PUBLICATION DATA

Balzac, Honoré de, 1799-1850.
 [Fille aux yeux d'or. English]
 The girl with the golden eyes / Honoré de Balzac ; translated
by Charlotte Mandell.
     p. cm. — (The art of the novella)
 ISBN-13: 978-0-9766583-1-3
 ISBN-10: 0-9766583-1-3
 I. Mandell, Charlotte. II, Title. III. Series.
 PQ2167.F5E5 2005
 843'.7—dc22

                                    2005033178

TO EUGÈNE DELACROIX, PAINTER

THE GIRL WITH THE GOLDEN EYES

One of the most appalling spectacles that exists is undoubtedly the general appearance of the Parisian population, a people horrible to see, gaunt, sallow, weather-beaten. Isn't Paris a vast field constantly whirled around by a hurricane of vested interests beneath which a monsoon of humans swirls about, whom death reaps more frequently than it does elsewhere? And aren't these humans always reborn just as tense as before, their faces contorted and twisted, divulging from every pore the thoughts, desires, and poisons their brains are obsessed with? Not faces, but masks—masks of weakness, masks of strength, masks of misery, masks of joy, masks of hypocrisy, all of them exhausted, all imprinted with the indelible signs of a panting greed. What do they want? Gold? Or pleasure?

Some observations about the soul of Paris might explain the causes for its cadaverous physiognomy that has only two ages—youth or caducity: a pallid, colorless youth, or a feeble decrepitude caked with makeup that tries to look young. Seeing this disinterred population, foreigners, if not enjoined to reflect, first of all experience a feeling of disgust for this capital, this immense workshop of sensual pleasures, which they themselves will soon no longer be able to leave, and where they will willingly remain to deform themselves. Few words suffice to give a physiological explanation for the almost hellish complexion of Parisian faces, for it isn't only in jest that Paris has been called a hell. Take this word literally. Here, everything smokes, burns, gleams, boils, blazes, evaporates, goes out, catches fire again, scatters sparks, crackles, and is consumed. Never before has life in any country been more fiery, or more ardent. The nature of this society that is always melting and reforming seems to say to itself after every work is finished, "Now on to the next one!"—just as Nature tells herself. Like Nature, this social nature concerns itself with insects, flowers of a day, trifles, ephemera, and also hurls fire and flames out from its eternal crater. Perhaps before we analyze the causes that produce a physiognomy peculiar to each tribe of this intelligent and mobile nation, we should point out the general cause that stains, blemishes, bruises, and darkens individuals more or less accordingly.

By dint of taking an interest in everything, the Parisian ends up being interested in nothing. Since no emotion predominates on his worn-out face, it turns grey as the walls of the houses, which have accumulated every kind of dust and smoke. In fact, indifferent today to what will intoxicate him tomorrow, the Parisian lives as a child does, no matter how old he is. He complains about everything, consoles himself for everything, makes fun of everything, forgets everything, wants everything, samples everything, takes everything with passion, abandons everything without concern—his kings, his conquests, his fame, or his idol, bronze or glass alike— in just the same way that he discards his stockings, his hats, and his fortune. In Paris, no sentimental attachment keeps things from being thrown away, and their constant movement makes for a struggle that relaxes passions: Here love becomes desire, and hatred a vague impulse. Here one has no relatives except the thousand-franc note, and no other friend but the pawnbroker. This general lack of concern bears fruit accordingly: Thus in the drawing room or in the street, no one is superfluous, no one is absolutely useful or absolutely harmful—idiots and rogues as well as men of wit and integrity. Here everything is tolerated, the government and the guillotine, religion and cholera. You can always fit into this world, you can never disappoint it. What is it, then, that rules in this world without customs, without beliefs, without sentiment, but where all sentiments, all beliefs, and all customs originate and terminate? Gold and pleasure. Take these two words as your lamp and travel all through this great plaster cage, this black-streaming beehive, and follow the serpentine twists of the thoughts that agitate it, lift it up, shape it. Look. First of all examine the people who have nothing.

The worker, the proletarian, the man who uses his feet, his hands, his tongue, his back, his arm alone, his five fingers in order to live. This one more than anyone else should economize on his vital principle, but instead exceeds his strength, yokes his wife to some machine, wears out his child and harnesses him to a wheel. His boss, the manufacturer, a sort of subsidiary string whose jerks move the workers, who with their dirty hands shape and gild porcelain, sew suits and dresses, temper iron, cut timber, forge steel, spin hemp and yarn, polish bronze, etch crystal, trace flowers, embroider wool, tame horses, plait harnesses and braids, trim copper, paint carriages, pollard old elms, steam cotton, treat cloth with sulfur, cut diamonds, buff metals, slice marble into slabs, polish stones, fashion thoughts, color, bleach, and dye everything—well, this subsidiary power has come to promise to this world of sweat, willpower, study, and patience, a high salary, either for the sake of the city's fashions, or on behalf of the monster named *speculation*. So these primates have set themselves to keeping watch, suffering, working, swearing, fasting, walking; all of them have gone beyond their own abilities, to earn this gold that bewitches them. Then, heedless of the future, greedy for pleasure, relying on their arms as the painter does on his palette, great lords for a day, they throw their Monday's earnings into cabarets, which form a belt of mud around the city; a girdle of the most shameless of Venuses, continually put on and taken off, where the periodic wealth of this people is lost as at gambling, a population as fierce in pleasure as it is calm at work. For five days, then, no rest for this active part of Paris! It gives itself up to impulses that warp it, make it gain weight, lose weight, turn pale, burst into a thousand spurts of creative willpower. Then its pleasure, its repose is a wearying debauchery, sallow of skin, black and blue from slaps, pallid from drunkenness, or yellow from indigestion, which lasts only two days, but which steals the future's bread, the week's soup, the wife's dresses, the baby's swaddling clothes, all in rags. These men, undoubtedly born to be handsome, for every living creature has his relative beauty, have enlisted, from early childhood, in the army of strength, the reign of the hammer, shears, spinning-machines, and have quickly vulcanized themselves. Vulcan, with his ugliness and his strength, is indeed the emblem of this ugly, strong nation, unequalled in mechanical intelligence, patient during working hours, terrible one day a century, inflammable as powder-shot, and prepared for the blaze of the revolution by brandy, spirited enough to catch fire from a specious word that, for this nation, always means: gold and pleasure! And including all those who hold out their hands for alms, for legitimate salaries, or for the five francs spent on all the various species of Parisian prostitution, or in fact for any rightly or ill-earned money, this people numbers three hundred thousand individuals. Without the cabarets, wouldn't the government be overthrown every Tuesday? Fortunately, on Tuesday, this people is dulled, has slept off its pleasure, has not a penny left, and returns to work, to dry bread, stimulated by a need for material reproduction that has become a habit for it. Nonetheless this people has its virtuous qualities, its Renaissance men, its unknown Napoleons, who are the classic examples of its strength carried to its highest expression, and who embody its social possibilities in an existence where thought and movement are combined less to imbue it with joy than to limit the effects of its suffering.

Fate made the workman thrifty, favored him with thought, which enabled him to set his mind towards the future; he meets a woman, finds he has become a father, and after several years of severe hardships starts a little dry goods store, rents a shop. If neither sickness nor vice stops him dead in his tracks, if he has prospered, this is an outline of his normal life.

Let us first of all salute this king of Parisian activity, who has mastered time and space. Yes, hail this creature composed of saltpeter and gas, who gives children to France during his laborious nights, and during the day multiplies his person for the service, glory, and pleasure of his fellow citizens. This man has solved the problem of being sufficient all at the same time for a loveable wife, his household, the paper *Le Constitutionnel*, his office, the National Guard, the Opéra, and God; but he is sufficient so that he can turn all of them into money—*Le Constitutionnel*, the office, the Opéra, the National Guard, his wife, and God. Let us salute this irreproachable multi-salaried worker. Awakened every day at five o'clock in the morning, like a bird he has crossed the space that separates his home from the Rue Montmartre. Despite thunder or wind, whether it's raining or snowing, he is at the *Constitutionnel* and waiting for the load of papers whose distribution is his responsibility. He receives this political bread with eagerness, takes it and carries it away. At nine o'clock in the morning, he is back home, joking with his wife; he steals a big kiss from her, swallows a cup of coffee or scolds his children. At quarter till ten, he is at the town hall. There, seated on his desk chair like a parrot on his perch, kept warm by the city of Paris, he inscribes the deaths and births of the whole arrondissement, without sparing a tear or a smile for them, until four o'clock in the afternoon. The happiness and unhappiness of the neighborhood pass under the nib of his pen, just as the spirit of the *Constitutionnel* had traveled earlier on his shoulders. Nothing weighs him down! He always goes straight in front of him, picks out his patriotism ready-made from the paper, contradicts no one, shouts or applauds with everyone, and lives like a swallow. Just a stone's throw from his parish, he can, in the event of an important ceremony, yield his desk to a supernumerary, and go sing a requiem under the pulpit of the church, where he is, on Sunday and feast days, the finest ornament, the most imposing voice, and where he energetically twists his wide mouth as he booms out a joyous *Amen*. He is a precentor. Freed at four o'clock from his official service, he appears in the heart of the most famous shop in the city to spread joy and cheer. Happy is his wife, since he doesn't have time to be jealous; he is rather a man of action than of sentiment. So as soon as he arrives, he teases the girls at the register, whose lively looks attract many a customer; delights at the finery, the scarves, the chiffon tailored by these skilful workers; or, even more often, before having dinner, he serves a customer, copies out a page of his cashbook, or sends the process-server to harass a delinquent debtor. At six o'clock every other day he is faithful to his role: A steady bass-baritone in the chorus, he can be found at the Opéra, ready to become a soldier, an Arab, a prisoner, a savage, a farmer, a ghost, the hoof of a camel, a lion, a devil, a genie, a slave, a black or white eunuch, always expert at showing joy, pain, pity, surprise, at letting out the requisite cries, at being quiet, at hunting, fighting, at representing Rome or Egypt; but always, to himself, he is just a haberdasher. At midnight, he once again becomes a good husband and man, a tender father, he slips into the conjugal bed, his imagination still preoccupied by the seductive forms of the nymphs at the Opéra, so that the world's depravities and La Taglioni's voluptuous dances all work for the benefit of conjugal love. Finally, if he sleeps, he sleeps quickly, and hurries his sleep just as he has hurried his life. Isn't it movement that makes man, man who is space embodied, the Proteus of civilization? This man sums up everything: history, literature, politics, government, religion, military arts. Isn't he a living encyclopedia, a huge atlas, continually at work, just like Paris, which never rests? He is all legs.

No physiognomy could keep itself pure in the service of such labors. Perhaps the worker who dies old at the age of thirty, his stomach tanned by progressive doses of his *eau-de-vie*, will be found, in the pronouncement of some prosperous philosophers, to be happier than the haberdasher is. One dies all at once and the other little by little. From his eight jobs, from his shoulders, from his throat, from his hands, from his wife and from his business, the haberdasher derives, as if from so many farms, some children, a few thousand francs, and the most laborious happiness that has ever refreshed the heart of a man. This wealth and these children, or the children who are everything to him, become prey to the superior world, to which he brings his money and his daughter, or his *lycée*-educated son, who, more learned than his father, aims his ambitions higher. Often the youngest son of a little retailer wants to be something in government.

This ambition raises our attentions to the second level of the Parisian spheres. Climb up one level and go to the mezzanine; or come down from the attic and stay on the fifth floor; either way, you enter the world that has something. Wholesale dealers and their helpers, employees, people who use small-business banks and have great probity, rogues, damned souls, high and low clerks, assistants to the bailiff, the solicitor, the notary public, finally the active, thinking, speculating members of this lower middle class who handle the interests of Paris and watch over its grain, supervise its foodstuffs, store the products made by the proletariat, pack the fruits of the Midi, the fish of the ocean, the wines of every hillside kissed by the sun; who stretch out their hands to the Orient and take shawls scorned by the Turks and Russians from it; who go all the way to the Indies to harvest crops, go to bed early to await sale, long for profit, discount their wares, circulate and collect all currencies; wrap up all Paris and sell it retail, wheel it in, are alert to any childish whim, spy out the caprices and vices of maturity, squeeze profit from disease. Even so, without drinking *eau-de-vie* like the workman, and without going to wallow in the mud of the city gates, they all thus overtax their strength; overstretch their bodies and morale, the former by means of the latter; desire dries them up, and they become lost in precipitate hurry. In them, physical torsion is accomplished under the whip of self-interest, under the scourge of ambitions that torment the elevated worlds of this monstrous city, just as the fortune of the proletariat is carried out under the cruel pendulum of material production ceaselessly demanded by the despotism of the aristocrat's *I want it.* Here too, to obey this universal master, pleasure or gold, you have to devour time, squeeze time, find more than twenty-four hours in the day and night, overwork, overdo everything, kill yourself, sell thirty years of old age for two years of unhealthy rest. But the worker dies in the hospital, when his last period of withering away has expired, whereas the man of the lower middle class persists in living and continues to live, but enfeebled: You will find him with a worn-out, flat, old face, dull eyes, weak legs, dragging himself along the boulevard—the girdle of his Venus, his beloved city—with a vacant look. What did this member of the bourgeoisie want? The saber of the National Guard, his dependable stew, a decent plot in the Père-Lachaise cemetery, and for his old age a little gold legitimately earned. His Monday is Sunday; his relaxation is a spin in the delivery van, a picnic in the country, during which his wife and children joyously swallow dust or roast themselves in the sun; his excursion is to some restaurant renowned for its poisonous dinners, or some family ball where you suffocate till midnight. Some simpletons are surprised at the St. Vitus's dance that seems to afflict the molecules seen through a microscope in a drop of water, but what would Rabelais' Gargantua say, figure of a sublime misunderstood audacity, what would this giant say, fallen from the celestial spheres, if he were to amuse himself contemplating the movement of this second level of Parisian life, one of whose formulae is presented here? Have you seen those little shacks, cold in summer, with no other hearth than a foot-warmer in winter, beneath the vast copper dome that tops the wheat market? Madame has been there since morning, she is manageress at the market and earns twelve thousand francs per year at this profession, they say. When Madame gets up in the morning, Monsieur goes into an ill-lit back room, where he makes short-term loans to merchants in his neighborhood. By nine o'clock he is at the passport office, where he is one of the chief clerks. At night he's at the ticket-office of the Théâtre Italien, or any other theater you like to name. The children are left in the care of the nanny, and later on they are sent to high school or boarding school. Monsieur and Madame live on the fourth floor, have only one stove, host dances in a twelve-by-eight-foot room illumined by oil lamps; but they give 150,000 francs to their daughter's dowry and retire at the age of fifty, when they begin to appear in the third-tier boxes at the Opéra, in a fiacre at

Longchamp, or in faded raiment, every sunny day, on the boulevards, the carefully tended fruit of all these labors. Respected in the neighborhood, well-regarded by the government, allied to the upper middle class, Monsieur obtains the Cross of the Legion of Honor at sixty-five years of age, and his son-in-law's father, the mayor of an arrondissement, invites him to his soirées. These labors of an entire lifetime thus benefit the children whom this lower middle class inevitably tries to lift to the upper middle class. Thus each sphere throws its entire spawn into the sphere above it. The son of the rich grocer is made a notary, the son of the lumber merchant becomes a magistrate. No cog misses its appointed groove, and everything stimulates the upward mobility of money.

Now we have reached the third circle of this hell, which might someday find its Dante. This third social circle is a kind of Parisian stomach, where the interests of the city are digested and where the crowd of attorneys, doctors, notaries, lawyers, businessmen, bankers, wholesale merchants, speculators, and magistrates are condensed in the form called *business affairs*, and where the mass is moved and stirred up by an acrid and venomous intestinal agitation. Here more than anywhere else are encountered causes for physical and moral destruction. Almost all these people live in squalid dens, in reeking courtrooms, in little barred offices, spending all day bent over beneath the weight of affairs; they get up at dawn to be prepared, to keep from being rooked, to win everything or to lose nothing, to seize hold of a man or of his money, to get a deal going or wrap one up, to take advantage of a fleeting circumstance, to have a man hanged or acquitted. They have an effect on their horses, work them to death, overtax them, aging their horses' legs long before their time. Time is their tyrant, they never have enough of it, it slips away from them; they can neither stretch it out nor contract it. What soul can remain great, pure, moral, generous, what face can remain handsome in the depraving exercise of a profession that forces you to bear the weight of public miseries, to analyze them, weigh them, gauge them, bleed them systematically? Where do these people keep their hearts? I don't know; but they leave them somewhere else, if they have any, before they descend every morning to the depths of the suffering that afflicts families. For them, there are no mysteries, they see the other side of the society for which they are confessors, and they despise it. Yet whatever they do, by dint of pitting themselves against corruption, they come to loathe it and are aggrieved by it; or else, out of weariness, by a secret transaction, they wed it. Ultimately, necessarily, they grow bored with all emotions, these people whom laws, people, institutions make fly down like crows onto corpses still warm. At any time of day, the money-man weighs the living, the contract-man weighs the dead, the law-man weighs our conscience. Obliged to talk continually, they replace ideas with words, emotions with phrases, and their soul turns into a larynx. They wear themselves down and grow demoralized. Neither the great negotiator, nor the judge, nor the lawyer keeps his heart in the right place: They stop feeling, they apply rules that bribes distort. Carried away by their torrential existence, they can be neither husbands nor fathers nor lovers; they glide on a sledge over the things of life, and live every minute compelled by the affairs of the great city. When they return home, they are called upon to attend a ball, or the Opéra, or parties where they go to develop clients for themselves, or acquaintances, or protectors. They all eat to excess, play, stay up late, till their faces grow round, smooth, red. To such terrible expenditures of intellectual strength, to such an increase in moral contradictions, they oppose not pleasure—too pale, flat, without contrast—but debauchery, a secret, terrifying debauchery, since they have everything at their disposal, and they are the ones that create society's morals. Their actual stupidity is hidden beneath an expert science. They know their profession, but they ignore anything unconnected with their profession. So, to protect their self-esteem, they call everything into question, criticize right and left; seem skeptical but are actually gullible, and drown their minds in interminable discussions. Almost all of them adopt convenient social, literary, or political prejudices so as to dispense with having to form an opinion of their own, just as they place their conscience in the shelter of common law, or of the commercial court. Having left home early in order to become remarkable men, they become mediocre, and crawl along on the heights of society. Accordingly, their faces present us with this sour pallor, these false complexions, these dull, lined eyes, these talkative and sensual mouths where the observer recognizes the symptoms of the degeneration of thought and its turning round and round in the dull circle of specialization that kills the generative faculties of the brain, the gift of seeing the big picture, of generalizing and deducing. They almost all shrivel up in the furnace of business affairs. Never can a man who has let himself be caught up in the crushing gears of these immense machines become great. If he is a doctor, either he has practiced little medicine, or he is an exception, a Bichat who dies young. If, as a great merchant, there's still something left, he is almost a financier like Jacques Coeur. Did Robespierre practice law? Danton was a lazy man who bided his time. But who in any case has ever envied the figures of Danton or Robespierre, superb as they may be? These busy men par excellence draw money to themselves and amass it in order to ally themselves with aristocratic families. If the worker's ambition is the same as a man of the lower middle class, here too passions are the same. In Paris, vanity epitomizes all the passions. The classic example of this level of society is either the ambitious bourgeois, who, after a life full of constant anxiety and maneuvering, gets onto the Council of State the way an ant crawls through a crack; or some newspaper editor, riddled with intrigues, whom the King makes a peer of France, perhaps to get back at the nobility; or some notary who gets to become mayor of his arrondissement: All of them have been exhausted by business affairs and, if they reach their goal, are *killed* doing so. In France, it is customary to honor grey hair. But Napoleon, Louis XIV, the truly great monarchs always wanted young people to carry out their plans.

Above this sphere lives the artistic world. But here again the faces, marked by the seal of originality, are sublimely broken, but broken they are, weary, haggard. Overwhelmed by the need to keep producing, overwhelmed by their costly imaginations, wearied by a devouring genius, starved for pleasure, the artists of Paris all want to recover through excessive labor the depletions left by laziness, and seek vainly to reconcile the world and glory, money and art. From the start, the artist is ceaselessly panting beneath the creditor; his needs engender debts, and his debts take his nights away from him. After work, pleasure. The actor plays till midnight, studies in the morning, rehearses at noon; the sculptor bends beneath his statue; the journalist is a thought on the march, like the soldier at war; the fashionable painter is overwhelmed with work, the painter without commissions is eaten away if he feels he is a man of genius. Competition, rivalries, calumnies murder talent. Some, desperate, roll into the abysses of vice, others die young and unknown because of having counted too soon on their future. Few of these faces, sublime to begin with, remain handsome. Moreover, the flamboyant beauty of their heads remains misunderstood. An artist's face is always extravagant, it is always above or below the conventional lines of what imbeciles call *ideal beauty*. What power destroys them? Passion. All passion in Paris is focused on two goals: gold and pleasure.

Now, can't you breathe more easily? Can't you feel that the spacious atmosphere has been purified? Here, no labor or suffering. The spiral of gold has reached the summit. From the bottom of basement windows where its rivulets begin, from the depths of shops where meager dykes constrain its flow, from the heart of neighborhood branch offices and big headquarters where it lets itself be made into bars, gold, in the form of dowries or inheritances, brought by the hands of young women or by the big-knuckled hands of old men, gushes towards the race of aristocrats where it gleams, spreads out, flows. But before we leave the four regions on which upper-class Paris relies, shouldn't we, after the aforementioned moral causes, deduce the physical causes, and call attention to a plague, which we could term as underlying, that is constantly acting on the faces of the porter, the shopkeeper, the laborer; shouldn't we point out a noxious influence whose corruptive power equals that of the Parisian administrators who complacently allow it to subsist! If the air of houses where most of the middle-class live is foul, if the atmosphere of the streets spits out cruel fumes in back-alley-shops where air is scarce, be aware that besides this pestilence, the 40,000 houses of this great city bathe their feet in ordure that the authorities have not yet seriously considered encircling with concrete walls that might prevent the most fetid mud from seeping through the ground, poisoning the wells, and continuing underground its famous name, Lutetia, place of the swamps. Half of Paris lies in the putrid exhalations of backyards, streets, and outhouses.

But now let us approach the grand, airy, gilded drawing-rooms, the mansions with gardens, the world of the rich and idle of private means. Here the faces are pallid, eaten away by vanity. Here there is nothing real. Doesn't the search for pleasure imply finding boredom? People in high society early on exhausted their true nature. Concerned only with creating joy for themselves, they quickly abused their senses, just as the common laborer abuses strong drink. Pleasure is like certain medicinal substances: To obtain the same effects, you have to keep increasing the dose, and death or mental exhaustion is inherent in the latter. All the lower classes lurk near the rich and keep an eye out for current tastes in order to exploit them and turn them into vices. How can one resist the clever seductions that are hatched in this country? Thus Paris has its *theriakis*, its own sort of opium-eaters— for them, gambling, gastrolatry, or the courtesan are their opium. So in these people you will see tastes but not passions—just romantic fantasies and timid affairs. Here impotence reigns; here there are no more ideas, the motive-force is lost in the playacting of the boudoir, in feminine antics. There are forty-year-old greenhorns, sixteen-year-old scholars. In Paris the rich encounter wit ready-made, pre-digested science, and opinions already formulated, which excuse them from having to have wit, science, or opinion. In this world, senselessness is as common as weakness and licentiousness. Here you become greedy for time by dint of losing it. Do not look for affection here any more than for ideas. Embraces mask profound indifference, politeness masks continuous scorn. Here the other is never loved. Shallow witticisms, hosts of indiscretions, much gossip, all blanketed by commonplaces—such is the substance of their language. But these unhappy "beautiful people" boast they don't get together in order to speak and create maxims in the manner of La Rochefoucauld; as if the eighteenth century had never discovered that happy medium between the too-full and absolute emptiness. If a few intelligent men make use of a subtle, deft witticism, it isn't understood. Soon they grow tired of giving without receiving, so they stay home and let idiots reign in their place. This hollow life, this constant waiting for a pleasure that doesn't come, this permanent boredom, this inanity of spirit, heart, and brain, this weariness of the great Parisian rout is reproduced in their features, and produces these cardboard faces, these premature wrinkles, this physiognomy of the rich where impotence scowls, where gold is reflected, and from which intelligence has fled.

This view of the moral Paris proves that the physical Paris could not be any different from the way it is. This tiara-clad city is a queen who, ever pregnant, has the usual irresistibly violent desires. Paris is the earth's head, an intelligence bursting with genius and leading human civilization, a great man, a continuously creative artist, a politician with second sight who must have a well-developed cerebrum, with all the vices of a great man, the fantasies of an artist, and the plainness of politics. Its physiognomy implies the germination of good and evil, struggle and victory; the moral battle of 1789 whose trumpets are still resounding throughout all the corners of the world, and also the defeat of 1814. Thus this city could not possibly be any more moral, or more cordial, or cleaner than the engine boiler of those magnificent pyroscaphs, the steamboats you admire cleaving the waves! Isn't Paris a sublime vessel freighted with intelligence? Yes, the city's coat of arms is one of those prophecies that fate sometimes allows itself. The City of Paris has its great mast of bronze, sculpted from victories, with Napoleon as its look-out. The carvel indeed pitches and rolls in the waves, but it travels the world, fires shells at it from the hundred mouths of its galleries, plows through the seas of science, scuds through them at full sail, shouts from the peak of its topsails in the voice of its scholars and artists: "Forward, onward! Follow me!" It carries an immense crew that loves to deck it out with fresh streamers. Cabin boys and street urchins laugh in the rigging; its ballast is the ponderous bourgeoisie, laborers and common tars; in its cabins, the happy passengers; elegant midshipmen smoke their cigars, leaning on the rails. Then on the upper deck, its soldiers, driven by exploration or ambition, will land on every shore, and, while spreading their lively luster, strive for a glory that is pleasure, or love affairs that need gold.

Hence the fierce impulses of the proletariat, hence the depraved interests that crush the lower and middle classes, hence the cruelties of the artist's thoughts, and the excesses of pleasure constantly sought by the upper class—all these explain the normal ugliness of Parisian physiognomy. Only in the Orient does the human race offer a magnificent countenance; but it is a result of the constant calm affected by those profound philosophers with their long pipes, little legs, and boxy torsos, who scorn movement and loathe it; whereas in Paris, the Petty, the Average, and the Great all run, jump, and caper about, whipped by the pitiless goddess, Need: need for money, fame, or fun. A fresh, restful, gracious, truly young face is the most extraordinary of exceptions here: It is rarely encountered. If you see such a one, it must either belong to a young and fervent curate, or to some good abbé in his forties, with a triple chin; or to a young individual of pure habits, such as might be bred in certain middle-class families; to a twenty-year-old mother, still full of illusions, breastfeeding her firstborn; to a green youngster newly arrived from the provinces, and confided to the care of a pious dowager who keeps him penniless; or perhaps to some shop boy, who goes to bed at midnight, tired out from folding or unfolding calico, and who gets up at seven in the morning to arrange the window display; or, often, to a man of science or poetry, who lives monastically in harmony with a sublime idea, who remains sober, patient, and chaste; or to some idiot, pleased with himself, feeding on stupidity, bursting with health, always smiling at himself; or to the happy and flaccid species of idlers, the only people truly happy in Paris, who every hour sample its shifting poesies.

Nonetheless, there is in Paris a company of privileged beings who profit from this extravagant movement of inventions, interests, business, arts, and gold. These beings are women. Although they too have a thousand secret causes that here, more than elsewhere, erode their physiognomy, one can find, in feminine society, little happy tribes who live in the oriental manner, and can preserve their beauty; but these women rarely show themselves on foot in the streets; they remain hidden, like rare plants that unfurl their petals only at certain times, and that constitute veritable exotic exceptions.

Yet Paris is essentially a land of contrasts. If true sentiments are rare here, one can also find, here as well as elsewhere, noble friendships, unbounded devotion. On this battlefield of interests and passions, just as in the midst of those societies on the march where egoism triumphs, where everyone is forced to defend himself alone, and that we call "armies," it seems that when feelings show themselves at all they have to be full-blown, and achieve nobility through contrast. So it is with faces. In Paris, sometimes, in the high aristocracy, a few ravishing faces of young men can be seen here and there, flowers of exceptional education and extraordinary manners. To the youthful beauty of English blood they join the firmness of southern traits, French wit, purity of form. The fire in their eyes, a delicious redness in their lips, the lustrous black of their fine hair, a fair complexion, the distinguished features of their face make them into beautiful human blossoms, magnificent to view above the mass of other dull, aged, crooked, grimacing physiognomies. Admire these young men with that greedy pleasure men take in looking at a pretty, decent, gracious individual, adorned with all the virginities with which our imagination likes to embellish the perfect girl.

If this glance swiftly directed at the population of Paris has made you realize the rarity of a face like Raphael, and the passionate admiration it must inspire there at first sight, the main purpose of our story will be justified. *Quod erat demonstrandum*, what there was to demonstrate has been shown, if we be allowed to apply scholarly phrases to the science of manners.

Now on one of those fine spring mornings—when the leaves are not yet green though they have unfurled, when the sun is beginning to make the roofs blaze and the sky is blue, when the Parisians emerge from their dens, come buzzing along on the boulevards, flow like a many-colored serpent along the Rue de la Paix towards the Tuileries to hail the nuptial rites that the countryside is celebrating once again—on one of those joyous days, then, a young man, handsome as the day itself, tastefully dressed, easy in his manners, and (we'll tell the secret) a love child, natural child of Lord Dudley and the famous Marquise de Vordac, was strolling down the wide lane of the Tuileries. This Adonis, named Henri de Marsay, was born in France, where Lord Dudley had come to marry off the young lady, already Henri's mother, to an old gentleman named M. de Marsay. This faded, almost extinct butterfly recognized the child as his own, in exchange for the usufruct of an income of 100,000 francs permanently granted his putative son; an extravagance that didn't cost Lord Dudley much: French bonds were then worth about seventeen francs fifty. The old gentleman died without having known his wife. Mme. de Marsay then married the Marquis de Vordac; but even before she became a marquise, she had not been all that concerned with her child or with Lord Dudley. To begin with, the war declared between France and England had separated the two lovers, and, in any case, fidelity was not and scarcely ever will be the fashion in Paris. And then the success of the elegant, pretty, universally adored woman drowned any maternal sentiment in the Parisian. Lord Dudley was no more concerned with his progeny than the mother was. The prompt infidelity of an ardently beloved young woman might perhaps have given him a sort of aversion for anything that came from her. Moreover, it might also be that fathers love only the children with whom they have become well acquainted; this is a social belief of the highest importance for a family's peace of mind, one that every bachelor should maintain, proving that paternity is only a sentiment raised in a hothouse by woman, customs, and laws.

Of the two men, poor Henri de Marsay knew a father only in the one not forced to be one. Naturally M. de Marsay's paternity was very incomplete. In the natural order of things, children have a father only at rare moments; and in this respect the gentleman imitated nature. The good man would not have sold his name if he hadn't had any vices. So he dined in dives without remorse and drank elsewhere the meager income the national treasury paid to men of private means. Then he handed the child over to an old sister, a maiden lady de Marsay, who took great care of him, and gave him, using the meager pension allotted by her brother, a private tutor, a priest without a penny or a stitch, who sized up the young man's future and resolved, out of the 100,000 francs allowance, to pay himself for the cares he devoted to his pupil, of whom he became fond. This private tutor one day found he had by chance become a genuine priest, one of those ecclesiastics cut out to become a cardinal in France, or a Borgia fit for the papal tiara. In three years he taught the child what they would have taken ten years to teach him in school. Then this great man, who was named the Abbé de Maronis, completed his student's education by having him study civilization in all its forms: He fed him from his own experience, hardly ever brought him into churches, which in those days were kept locked; sometimes took him backstage in theaters, more often to the homes of courtesans; he took apart human emotions piece by piece for him; taught him politics in the heart of salons, where it was cooking; he explicated for him the machinery of government, and tried, out of friendship for a fine neglected nature, but one rich in hope, to serve as a virile replacement for the mother: Isn't the Church the mother of orphans? His student responded well to so many attentions. This worthy man died a bishop in 1812, with the satisfaction of having left beneath heaven a child whose heart and mind were so well formed at sixteen years of age, that he could easily get the upper hand of a man of forty. Who would have expected to meet a heart of bronze, an unfeeling brain beneath so seductive an exterior, like those that the painters of old, those naïve artists, gave to the serpent in the earthly paradise? That was still not enough. The good purple devil had also introduced his favorite child to certain acquaintances in high Parisian society who would be the equivalent, in the young man's hands, of another 100,000 in income. Finally, this priest, lecherous but political, unbelieving but knowledgeable, treacherous but likeable, weak in appearance but as vigorous of mind as he was of body, was so truly useful to his student, so indulgent towards his vices, such a good calculator of every kind of strength, so profound when some kind of human deduction had to be made, so fresh at table, at Frascati's gaming rooms, at... I don't know where else, that the grateful Henri de Marsay was now, by 1814, scarcely moved by anything but the sight of the portrait of his dear bishop, the only personal belonging this prelate was able to bequeath to him. The bishop was an admirable example of the men whose genius will save the Catholic, Apostolic, and Roman church, which is at the moment compromised by the weakness of its recruits, and by the old age of its pontiffs; but so the Church wishes it. The continental war prevented the young de Marsay from meeting his true father, whose name it is doubtful he even knew. An abandoned child, he didn't know Mme de Marsay either. Naturally he barely missed his putative father. As to Mlle. de Marsay, his only mother, he had a pretty little tomb raised to her in the Père Lachaise Cemetery when she died. Monseigneur de Maronis had guaranteed one of the best places in heaven to this old maid, so that, seeing her happy to die, Henri gave her egotistical tears and began to cry for himself. Seeing this suffering, the abbé dried the tears of his student, pointing out to him that the good lady took her snuff in such a disgusting way, and had become so ugly, so deaf, and so boring, that he should be grateful to death. The bishop had had his student set free in 1811. Then when the mother of M. de Marsay married again, the priest chose, in a family council, one of those honest brainless men picked out by him from the confessional, and charged him with administering the fortune whose income he did indeed apply to the needs of the community, but whose capital he wanted to preserve.

Near the end of 1814, then, Henri de Marsay had no remaining obligatory sentiment left on Earth, and found himself as free as a bird without a mate. Although he had completed his twenty-second year, he looked as if he were scarcely seventeen. Even his severest rivals regarded him as the prettiest boy in Paris. From his father, Lord Dudley, he had acquired the most amorously seductive blue eyes; from his mother, the thickest black hair; from them both, a pure blood, the skin of a young girl, a gentle, modest bearing, a slim, aristocratic waist, beautiful hands. For a woman, to see him was to be crazy about him; you know how it is—she conceives of one of those desires that gnaws at her heart, but that is soon forgotten thanks to the impossibility of satisfying it, because the woman is one of the common Parisian variety without tenacity. Few of them say to themselves the I WILL PREVAIL of the men of the House of Orange. Beneath this youthful bloom, and despite the limpid pool of his eyes, Henri had a lion's courage, a monkey's dexterity. He could slice through a bullet with a knife blade ten paces away; rode horseback in a way that fulfilled the myth of the centaur; gracefully drove a long-reined carriage; was agile as Cherubino and calm as a lamb; but he could beat a man from the slums at the horrid sports of kick-boxing or quarterstaff. He had such a way with the piano that he could become an artist if he fell into misfortune, and had a voice that would have been worth 50,000 francs a season to a tenor like Barbaja. Alas, all these fine qualities, these charming defects, were tarnished by a horrible vice: He believed in neither men nor women, neither God nor the devil. Nature had begun to endow him with capriciousness; a priest had completed the process.

To make the present adventure understandable, it is necessary to add here that Lord Dudley naturally found many women willing to produce a few copies from such a charming portrait. His second masterpiece of this sort was a young girl named Euphémie, born to a Spanish lady, raised in Havana, and brought back to Madrid with a young Creole woman from the Antilles, with all the ruinous tastes of the colonies; but she was fortunately married to an old and powerfully rich Spanish lord, Don Hijos, Marquis de San-Réal, who, after the occupation of Spain by French troops, had come to live in Paris, and had a house on the Rue Saint-Lazare. As much by unconcern as out of respect for the innocence of youth, Lord Dudley never bothered to inform his children about the various kinships he was creating for them everywhere. This is a slight inconvenience of civilization, which has many advantages; one must overlook its drawbacks in favor of its benefits. Lord Dudley, to finish with him, came in 1816 to take refuge in Paris, in order to avoid the pursuits of English justice, which protects nothing but merchandise from the Orient. When he saw Henri, the traveling lord asked who this young man was. Then, hearing his name, he said, "Ah! He is my son. What a pity!"

That is the story of the young man who, around the middle of April, in 1815, was nonchalantly strolling down the wide lane in the Tuileries, like all animals who, knowing their strength, walk in peace and majesty; ordinary people naively turned around to look at him again, women didn't turn round at all, they waited for him on his return, and engraved this suave face—which wouldn't have marred the body of the most beautiful of them—in their memory, so as to be able to recall him at the right time.

"What are you doing here on a Sunday?" the Marquis de Ronquerolles asked Henri in passing.

"There are fish in the net," the young man replied.

This exchange of thoughts was made by means of two significant glances, without either Ronquerolles or de Marsay seeming to recognize each other. The young man examined the people strolling by, with that swiftness of glance and keen sense of hearing peculiar to the Parisian who seems, at first glance, to see nothing and hear nothing, but who sees and hears everything. At that instant, a young man came up to him, took him familiarly by the arm, and said, "How are things, my good de Marsay?"

"Splendid," de Marsay replied with that seemingly affectionate air which between the young people of Paris proves nothing, either for now or for the future.

In fact, the youth of Paris are like none of the youth in other cities. They are divided into two classes: the young man who has something, and the young man who has nothing; or the young man who thinks and the one who spends. But you must understand that here it is a question only of those native sons who live the grand style of elegant life in Paris. A few other kinds of young men do exist, but they are children who come late to the Parisian way of life, and remain fooled by it. They don't speculate, they study; they cram, say the others. Finally there are still other sorts of young men, both rich and poor, who embrace careers and follow them quite simply; they are a little like Rousseau's Émile, an ordinary citizen through and through, and they never belong to society. Diplomats impolitely call them simpletons. Simpletons or not, they increase the number of those average people beneath whose weight France bends. They are always there; always ready to spoil public or private affairs with the flat trowel of mediocrity, boasting about their impotence, which they call manners and probity. These Good Conduct Medals infest the government, the army, the magistracy, the chambers, the court. They weaken, depress the country as it were, and form in the body politic a lymph that overburdens it and makes it flabby.

These respectable individuals call talented people immoral, or rogues. Though these rogues get paid for their services, at least they serve; while the "respectable" people do nothing but harm, but are respected by the crowd. Fortunately for France, though, elegant youth firmly stigmatizes them with the name of "old fools."

Hence, at first glance, it is natural to regard the two kinds of young men who lead an elegant life—an enviable guild to which Henri de Marsay belonged—as quite distinct. But observers who do not stop at the surface of things are soon convinced that the differences are purely moral, and that nothing is so deceptive as their attractive shell. These young men all hasten to override everyone else; blather about things, people, literature, the fine arts; always have the "Pitt and Cobourg" of that year on the tips of their tongues; interrupt conversation with a pun; poke fun at science and scholars; scorn everything they don't know or fear—then set themselves above everything, appointing themselves supreme judges of everything. All of them would willingly cheat their fathers, and would be ready to gush crocodile tears onto their mothers' breast; but in fact they don't believe in anything; they speak ill of women, or play at being chaste, actually all the while obeying an evil courtesan, or some old socialite. All of them are eaten away down to their very bones by calculation, depravity, by a brutal desire to succeed, and if they are in danger of suffering from the stone, if you examine them you will find each does have one, but in their hearts. In their normal state, they have the prettiest exteriors, swear on their friendship every other minute, and are thoroughly engaging. The same mockery dominates their ever-changing jargon; they aim for eccentricity in their appearance, revel in repeating the silly phrases of whatever actor is in vogue, and start out any new acquaintance with scorn or impertinence so that they can somehow score the first point in this game: But woe betide anyone who doesn't know enough to let one of his eyes be gouged out so he can gouge out both of theirs! They seem just as indifferent to the misfortunes of their country as they are to its scourges. They are all like the pretty white foam that crowns waves in storms. They get dressed, dine, dance, have fun on the day of the Battle of Waterloo, during the cholera, or during a revolution. Finally, they all make the same expenditures; but here the difference begins. Of this fluctuating and pleasantly squandered fortune, some have the capital, and others are waiting for it; they have the same tailors, but the bills of the second kind of youth are yet to be settled. If some, like sieves, receive all kinds of ideas without keeping any of them, the second kind compare them and take all the good ones for themselves. If the former think they know something, but actually know nothing and understand everything, lend everything to those who need nothing and offer nothing to those who need something, the latter secretly study the thoughts of other people, and invest their money as well as their whims at high interest. The former have ceased to receive true impressions, since their soul, like a mirror tarnished with use, no longer reflects any image; the latter economize their senses and their life, all the while seeming to throw them both out the window. The former, based on the faith of hope, devote themselves without conviction to a system that is borne forth by a fair wind, but then they jump onto another political craft when the first one starts to go adrift; the latter size up the future, sound it, and see in political loyalty what the English see in commercial probity: an ingredient for success. But where the young man who has something makes a play on words or utters a fine turn of phrase about the change of thrones, the one who has nothing makes a public calculation, or a secret servile act, and succeeds, all the while showering his friends with punches. The former never believe in the abilities of others, take all their ideas as new, as if the world had just been created overnight; they have a limitless confidence in themselves, and have no enemy crueler than their own person. But the latter are armed with a continual mistrust of men, whom they value at their true worth, and are just profound enough to have one more thought than the friends they exploit; and at night, when their head is resting on the pillow, they weigh men as a miser weighs his gold coins. The former get angry at an impertinent remark of no importance, and let themselves be made fun of by diplomats who make them pose in front of them while they hold the string of these marionettes, self-esteem; whereas the latter earn the respect of others and choose their victims and their protectors.

Then, one day, the ones who had nothing, have something; and the ones who had something, have nothing. They regard their comrades who have attained a position as sly little devils, with their hearts in the wrong place, but also as strong men. "He is very strong!" is the immense praise awarded those who have succeeded, *quibuscumque viis*, by whatever means, in politics, or with a woman, or a fortune. Among them, we find certain young men who play this role starting out with debts; and naturally, they are more dangerous than those who play it without having a penny.

The young man who called himself a friend of Henri de Marsay was a scatterbrain, fresh out of the provinces, whom the young men then in fashion were teaching the art of properly squandering an inheritance; but he had one last piece of pie left to eat in his province, a reliable estate. He was simply an heir who had gone without transition from his meager hundred francs a month to the entire paternal fortune, and who, even if he didn't have wit enough to see that people were making fun of him, knew enough math to confine himself to two-thirds of his capital. He was just discovering in Paris, in return for a few thousand-franc bills, the exact price of equestrian tack, the art of not taking too much care of his gloves, of listening to expert meditations on what wages to give people, and finding out what fixed sum was the most profitable to settle on with them; he was most eager to be able to talk knowledgeably about his horses or his dog from the Pyrénées, and to recognize what sort of woman a lady was by recognizing her attire, her walk, and her boots; studying the rules of *écarté*, remembering a few fashionable phrases, and, by means of his stay in Parisian society, acquiring the necessary authority to import a taste for tea and English silver later on into the provinces, and to give himself the right to scorn everything around him for the rest of his days. De Marsay had taken him on as a friend to make use of him in society, the way a bold speculator uses a trusted assistant. The false or real friendship of de Marsay gave social position to Paul de Manerville who, for his part, thought he was cunning in thus exploiting his close friend. He lived in his friend's reflection, constantly sheltered under his umbrella, wore the same shoes as he did, basked in his glow. Standing next to Henri, or even walking alongside him, he seemed to be saying: "Don't insult us, we are real tigers." Often he allowed himself to say self-complacently: "If I asked Henri for such or such a thing, he is a good enough friend of mine to do it...." But he took care never to ask him for anything. He was afraid of him, and his fear, though imperceptible, reacted on others, and was of service to de Marsay. "What a proud man de Marsay is," Paul would say. "You'll see, he'll be whatever he wants to be. I wouldn't be surprised to find him someday as Minister of Foreign Affairs. Nothing can resist him." So he made de Marsay into what Corporal Trim made of his hat, a constant byword. "Ask de Marsay, and you'll see!"

Or else: "The other day, de Marsay and I were out hunting, he didn't want to believe me, but I jumped a bush without budging an inch from my horse!"

Or else: "The other day, de Marsay and I were visiting some ladies, and, my word of honor, I was..." and so on.

So Paul de Manerville could only be classified among the great, illustrious, and powerful tribe of simpletons who achieve success. He would be a deputy one day. Right now he wasn't even a young man yet. His friend de Marsay defined him thus: "You ask me what Paul is. Paul? Paul is Paul de Manerville."

"I'm surprised, old man," he said to de Marsay, "that you're here, on Sunday."

"I was going to ask you the same thing."

"An affair?"

"Possibly...."

"Nonsense!"

"I could easily say just the same to you, without compromising my own amour. Anyway a woman who comes to the Tuileries on Sunday is of no consequence, aristocratically speaking."

"Ha!"

"Be quiet, or I won't tell you anything else. You laugh too loudly, you'll make people think we overdid it at lunch. Last Thursday, here, on the Feuillants esplanade, I was strolling along without thinking about anything at all. But when I had reached the gate to the Rue de Castiglione through which I planned to leave, I found myself face to face with a woman, or rather a young lady who, if she didn't exactly throw her arms around my neck, still found herself halted, stopped dead—less, I think, out of human respect than through one of those profound shocks that numb your arms and legs, travel down your spine, and end in the soles of your feet, rooting you to the ground. I have often produced effects of this sort, a kind of animal magnetism that becomes intense when both parties feel interconnected. But, dear friend, I was not drunk, and she was not an ordinary tart. Psychologically speaking, her face seemed to say: 'What, you're here, my ideal, the being from my innermost thoughts, my dreams morning and night? How can you be? Why this morning? Why not yesterday? Take me, I'm yours, *et cetera*!' 'Oh good,' I said to myself, 'another one!' So I examined her. Ah! Dear friend, physically speaking, this stranger is the most delightfully feminine woman I have ever met. She belongs to that variety of female the Romans called *fulva, flava*, a woman of fire. And what struck me first of all, what I'm still smitten with, are her two yellow eyes, like tiger's eyes; a golden yellow that gleams, living gold, gold that thinks, gold that loves and wants more than anything to come nestle inside your watch-pocket!"

"But we know all about that, old man!" Paul exclaimed. "She comes here sometimes, she's the Girl with the Golden Eyes. We gave her that name. She's a young lady about twenty-two years old, and I've seen her here when the Bourbons were here, but with a woman who's worth 100,000 times more than she is."

"Shut up, Paul! It's impossible for any woman whatsoever to surpass this girl who's like a cat who wants to come rubbing up against your legs, a pale girl with ash blond hair, delicate in her looks, but with fine hairs on the third phalanx of her fingers; and her cheeks are covered with a white down, luminous on a sunny day, which begins at the ears and disappears down her neck."

"Oh! But the other one, my dear de Marsay! She has black eyes that have never cried, but burn; black eyebrows that meet and give her a look of hardness that's contradicted by the full contours of her lips, on which no kiss remains—passionate, fresh lips; a Moorish complexion by which a man can be warmed like the sun; but, my word of honor, she looks just like you...."

"You flatter her!"

"An arched waist, the streamlined waist of a racing sloop, which pounces on a merchant vessel with a French impetuosity, overtakes it and makes it go under in no time."

"Come on, old man, what do I have to do with a woman I've never even seen!" de Marsay interrupted. "As long as I've been studying women, my unknown girl is the only one whose virgin breast, passionate and voluptuous forms, have actualized for me the only woman I've ever dreamt of! She is the original of the rapturous painting called

"The Woman Caressing Her Chimera," the most ardent, infernal inspiration of ancient genius, a holy form of poetry prostituted by those who copied it for frescoes and mosaics, for a bunch of bourgeois who see nothing in this cameo but a bracelet charm, and put it on the covers of their pocket-watches, whereas it is everything that a woman is, an abyss of pleasures you wallow in without ever finding an end to them, yet it's an ideal woman who can sometimes actually be seen in Spain or Italy, almost never in France. Well, I've seen this Girl with the Golden Eyes again, this woman caressing her chimera, I saw her here, on Friday. I sensed she would return the next day at the same time. I was not wrong. I took pleasure in following her without her seeing me, in studying the indolent walk of an idle woman, in whose movements you can discern a sleeping voluptuousness. Well, she turned around, saw me, again adored me, again trembled, shivered. Then I noticed the veritable Spanish *duenna* guarding her, a hyena whom some jealous man dressed up as a woman, some female devil well-paid to guard this suave creature.... Oh! Then the duenna made me even more than in love—she made me curious. Saturday, no one. Here I am, today, waiting for this girl whose chimera I am, and asking for nothing better than to pose like the monster in the fresco."

"There she is," Paul said, "everyone's turning around to look at her...."

The unknown girl blushed; her eyes sparkled when she saw Henri. Lowering them, she passed by.

"You think she noticed you?" Paul de Manerville cried amusedly.

The duenna observed the two young men fixedly and attentively. When the unknown girl and Henri met again, the young girl brushed by him, and squeezed the young man's hand with her own. Then she turned back and smiled passionately; but the duenna pulled her along at a fast pace towards the gate to the Rue Castiglione. The two friends followed the young woman, admiring the magnificent sinuosity of her neck, to which her head was joined by a coordination of vigorous lines, whence a few little ringlets of hair forced their way out. The Girl with the Golden Eyes had the thin, well-turned ankle that offers so many attractions to ready imaginations. She was elegantly shod, and wore a short dress. During her promenade, she turned round from time to time to look again at Henri, and seemed only regretfully to follow the older woman, of whom she seemed to be both mistress and slave: She could have her thrashed black and blue, but could not have sent her away. So much was obvious. The two friends reached the gate. Two footmen in livery folded down the steps of a tasteful carriage adorned with a coat of arms. The Girl with the Golden Eyes climbed in first, took the side where she would be seen when the car turned around; put her hand on the door and waved her handkerchief, without the duenna knowing, mocking the *whatever will they say* of curious onlookers, and publicly saying to Henri with the motions of her handkerchief: "Follow me...."

"Have you ever seen anyone motion more nicely with a handkerchief?" Henri said to Paul de Manerville.

Then, noticing a fiacre ready to go after having discharged its passengers, he signed to the cabman to stop.

"Follow that carriage, mark the street and house it turns into, you'll have ten francs.—Goodbye, Paul."

The fiacre followed the carriage. The carriage returned to the Rue Saint-Lazare, to one of the most beautiful mansions in the neighborhood.

De Marsay wasn't stupid. Any other young man would have obeyed the wish to find out some more information about a girl who so well embodied the most luminous ideas expressed about women in Oriental poetry; but, too skilful thus to compromise the future of his love affair, he just told his fiacre to continue on the Rue Saint-Lazare and bring him back to his house. The next day, his chief valet-de-chambre, Laurent, a boy as crafty as a Frontin out of the old comedies, waited near the house inhabited by the unknown girl at the hour when the mail was delivered. In order to be able to spy at his ease and wander around the mansion, he had, following the habit of policemen who want to disguise themselves, provided himself with the outfit of a peasant from the Auvergne, and tried to make his face look the part. When the mailman who was making the deliveries that morning for the Rue Saint-Lazare came by, Laurent pretended to be a messenger who was having trouble remembering the name of a person to whom he was supposed to deliver a package, and consulted the mailman. Deceived first of all by appearances—the sight of such a picturesque person in the midst of Parisian civilization—the postman told him that the mansion where the Girl with the Golden Eyes lived belonged to Don Hijos, Marquis de San-Réal, a Spanish grandee. Naturally the Auvergnat had no business with the marquis.

"My package," he said, "is for the Marquise."

"She is away," the mailman replied. "Her letters are forwarded to London."

"So the Marquise isn't a young lady who..."

"Aha!" said the mailman, interrupting the valet-de-chambre and looking at him attentively, "you're a messenger like I can fly."

Laurent displayed a few gold coins to the functionary, who began to smile.

"Look, here's the name of your prey," he said, taking out of his leather box a letter that bore a London stamp, and on which was this address:

> *To Mademoiselle*
> PAQUITA VALDÈS,
> *Rue Saint-Lazare, Hôtel de San-Réal,*
> PARIS.

was written in the tiny, elongated letters of a woman's hand.

"Would you be hostile to a bottle of Chablis, accompanied by a steak sautéed with mushrooms, and preceded by a few dozen oysters?" Laurent said, who wanted to conquer the precious friendship of the mailman.

"At 9:30, after work. Where?"

"At the corner of the Rue de la Chaussée-d'Antin and the Rue Neuve-des-Mathurins, 'Au Petit Sans Vin,'" said Laurent.

"Listen, friend," the mailman said when he joined the valet, an hour after that first meeting, "if your master is in love with this girl, he's got his work cut out for him! I doubt you'll be able to see her. In the ten years I've been a mailman in Paris, I've been able to study quite a few different security systems! But I can honestly say, without fear of being refuted by any of my comrades, that there is no gate as mysterious as M. de San-Réal's. No one can penetrate the house without some sort of password, and notice that the house was chosen on purpose between a courtyard and a garden, to avoid any communication with other houses. The guard is an old Spaniard who never speaks a word of French, but who stares hard at people, the way the secret agent Vidocq would, to make sure they're not thieves. Even if this head clerk let himself be tricked by a lover, a thief, or by you (no offense), well, in the first room, which is closed off by a glass door, you'd meet a majordomo surrounded by lackeys, an old joker even more savage and surly than the guard. If someone gets through the carriage entrance, my majordomo emerges, makes you wait under the peristyle, and puts you through an interrogation as if you were a criminal. That has happened to me, an ordinary mailman. He took me for a *seminary* in disguise," he said, laughing at his own play on the word 'emissary.' "As to other people, don't even hope to get anything out of them, I think they're mute, no one in the neighborhood has heard a word out of them; I don't know what kind of wages they're given not to speak and not to drink anything; the fact is they're unapproachable, either because they're afraid of being shot, or because they have an enormous amount to lose if they're indiscreet. If your master loves Mlle.

Paquita enough to surmount all these obstacles, he will certainly not triumph over Doña Concha Marialva, the duenna who is her companion, and who would put her under her skirts rather than leave her. These two women seem as if they're sewn together."

"What you tell me, worthy mailman," Laurent said after tasting the wine, "confirms what I've just learned. On my word as an honest man, I thought they were making fun of me. The greengrocer across the street told me that at night, in the gardens, they let loose some dogs whose food is hung from posts, so that they can't reach it. So these cursed animals think that any people who come in are after their food, and they'd tear them to pieces. You might suggest I throw them lumps of meat, but apparently they're raised to eat only from the concierge's hand."

"The porter of M. le Baron de Nucingen, whose garden is next door to that of the San-Réal mansion, told me the exact same thing," the mailman said.

"Oh good, my master knows him," Laurent told himself. "Did you know," he resumed, keeping a careful eye on the mailman, "that I belong to a master who is a proud man, and if he got it into his head to kiss the soles of an empress's feet, that would inevitably come to pass? If he needed you, which I hope for your sake is the case, since he's generous, could we count on you?"

"Indeed, Monsieur Laurent. My name is Moinot. My name is written exactly the same as *moineau*, sparrow: M-o-i-n-o-t."

"I see," said Laurent.

"I live on the Rue des Trois-Frères, No. 11, on the sixth floor," Moinot went on. "I have a wife and four children. If what you want from me doesn't go beyond the possibilities of conscience and my administrative duties—you understand!—I am yours to command."

"You are a good man," Laurent said to him as he shook his hand.

"Paquita Valdès must be the mistress of the Marquis de San-Réal, a friend of King Ferdinand's. Only an eighty-year-old Spanish cadaver is capable of taking such precautions," Henri said when his valet de chambre had told him the results of his researches.

"Monsieur," Laurent said to him, "unless you arrive there in a balloon, no one can get into that mansion."

"How stupid you are! Does one need to enter the mansion to have Paquita, when Paquita can easily leave it?"

"But, Monsieur, what about the duenna?"

"We can confine her to her room for a few days, your duenna."

"So then, we'll have Paquita!" Laurent said, rubbing his hands.

"Idiot!" Henri continued. "I'll condemn you to the Concha if you push insolence to the point of talking that way about a woman before I've had her. Turn your mind to dressing me, I'm going out."

Henri remained for a moment plunged in joyous thought. We'll say this in praise of women: He won all those he deigned to desire. And what could one think of a woman without a lover who could resist a young man armed with beauty, which is the body's spirit, armed with spirit, which is the soul's grace, armed with moral force and wealth, which are the only two real powers? But by triumphing so easily, de Marsay was bound to become bored with his triumphs, so that for about two years he was often bored. Plunging to the depths of sensual delights, he brought back more pebbles than pearls. Thus he had come to the point, as sovereigns do, of begging Fortune for some obstacle to conquer, some undertaking that asked for the deployment of his idling moral and physical strength. Although Paquita Valdès presented him with the marvelous assembly of perfections he had not yet enjoyed in detail, the attraction of passion was almost nil for him. A constant satiety had weakened the sentiment of love in his heart. Like the old and the blasé, he had nothing left but extravagant whims, ruinous tastes, and fantasies that, once satisfied, left him with no good memories in his heart. In young people, love is the finest of sentiments, it makes life blossom in the soul, by its sun-like power it spreads the fairest inspirations and their great thoughts: The beginnings of any affair have a delicious taste. In men, love becomes a passion: Force leads to abuse. In old men, it turns to vice: Impotence leads to excess. Henri was at once an old man, a man, and a young man. For him to have the emotions of true love, he needed someone like Lovelace's Clarissa Harlowe. Without the magical reflection of such an elusive pearl, he could experience nothing more than either passions sharpened by some Parisian vanity, or wagers made with himself to cause some woman to sink to a degree of corruption, or adventures that stimulated his curiosity. The report of Laurent, his valet, had just given an enormous value to the Girl with the Golden Eyes. It was a matter of waging battle with some secret enemy, who seemed as dangerous as he was cunning; to earn victory, all the forces at Henri's disposal would be needed. He was going to play the ancient eternal comedy that will always be new, whose characters are an old man, a young lady, and a lover: Don Hijos, Paquita, de Marsay. Though Laurent was as good as Figaro, the duenna seemed incorruptible. Thus, the real-life play was more formidably developed by chance than it had ever been by any dramatic author! But isn't Chance also a person of genius?

"We'll have to play a close game," Henri told himself.

"Well, then," Paul de Manerville said to him as he came in, "where are we now? I've come to lunch with you."

"Fine," Henri said. "You won't be shocked if I complete my toilette in front of you?"

"What a funny thought!"

"We're borrowing so many things from the English nowadays that we might turn into hypocrites and prudes just like them," Henri said.

Laurent had brought so many implements to his master, so many different articles, and such pretty ones, that Paul couldn't prevent himself from exclaiming: "What, is your toilette going to take two hours?"

"Not at all," Henri said, "two and a half hours."

"Well, since we're alone and we say anything we like to each other, explain to me why such a superior man as yourself—for you are superior—affects this exaggerated vanity, which must not be natural in you. Why spend two and a half hours grooming yourself, when it's enough to take a fifteen-minute bath, run a comb through your hair, and get dressed? Come now, tell me your system."

"I'd have to like you a lot, you fat oaf, to confide such high thoughts to you," the young man said, who at that moment was having his feet scrubbed with a soft brush lathered with English soap.

"But I've vowed the most sincere attachment to you," Paul de Manerville replied, "and I like you so much that I think you're even better than I am!"

"You must have noticed, if you're still capable of observing a moral fact, that women like vain men," de Marsay continued, responding to Paul's declaration with a meaningful glance. "Do you know why women like vain men? My friend, conceited men are the only men who take care of themselves. Now, doesn't taking excessive care of yourself imply that you're looking after the good of the other person in yourself? The man who doesn't belong to himself is precisely the man women are fond of. Love is essentially a thief. I'm not talking about that excess of cleanliness they're crazy about. Have you ever found a woman who was passionately in love with a slovenly person, even one who was a remarkable man? If ever such a thing occurred, we'd have to attribute it to the whims of a pregnant woman, those weird ideas that come into her head and are told to everyone without a second thought. On the contrary, I have seen remarkable people quite simply dropped because of their negligence. A vain man who takes care of his appearance is one who takes care of a foolish thing, mere trifles. And what is woman? A mere trifle, an ensemble of foolish things. With two words spoken into the air, can't we make her work for four hours? She is certain the vain man will take care of her, since he doesn't think about big things. She will never play second fiddle to fame, ambition, politics, art, those big public girls who she thinks of as her rivals. Further, vain men have the courage to cover themselves with ridicule to please a woman, and her heart is full of consideration for a man who is made ridiculous by love. Finally, a conceited man can only be conceited if he has some reason to be so. Women are the ones who give us this rank. The conceited man is the colonel of love, he has affairs, he has his regiment of women to command! My dear friend! In Paris, everything is known, and a man cannot be conceited here *gratis*. You who have only one woman and who may have reason to have only one, if you tried to seem full of yourself, you'd not only become ridiculous, you'd be dead. You'd become a walking caricature, one of those men inevitably condemned to do one single thing. You would signify *foolishness* the way M. de Lafayette signifies America; M. de Talleyrand, diplomacy; Désaugiers, song; M. de Ségur, romance. If they depart from their specialty, everyone stops believing in the value of what they do. That's what we're like in France, always supremely unfair! M. de Talleyrand might be a great financier, M. de Lafayette a tyrant, and Désaugiers an administrator. You could have forty women the following year, but publicly they wouldn't credit you with even one. Thus conceit, my friend Paul, is the sign of an unquestionable power acquired over the female population. A man loved by many women passes for having superior qualities; and then he can have whomever he likes, the wretch! But do you think it's nothing to have the right to come into a salon, survey everyone there from over your cravat or through a monocle, and be able to scorn the most superior man there if he's wearing an outdated waistcoat? Laurent, you're hurting me! After lunch, Paul, we'll go to the Tuileries to see the adorable Girl with the Golden Eyes."

When, after an excellent meal, the two young men had paced up and down the Feuillants terrace and the wide lane in the Tuileries, they didn't meet the sublime Paquita Valdès anywhere, on whose account fifty of the most elegant young men in Paris were there, all perfumed with musk, wearing cravats, boots, spurs, using their riding crops, walking, talking, laughing, telling everyone to go to the devil.

"Bullseye!" Henri said, "the most excellent idea in the world has just come to me. This girl gets letters from London, so we have to buy or bribe the mailman, open a letter, read it of course, then slip a little *billet doux* into it, and seal it back up. The old tyrant, *crudel tiranno*, must know the person who writes the letters that come from London, and doesn't distrust them."

The next day, de Marsay came again to stroll in the sun on the Feuillants terrace, and saw Paquita Valdès there: Already passion had made her grow even more beautiful to him. He completely lost his head over those eyes whose rays seemed to have the nature of the sun's, and whose ardor epitomized that of her perfect body, seat of voluptuous delight. De Marsay was burning to brush against the dress of this seductive girl when they met in their walk; but his attempts were always in vain. When he had passed the duenna and Paquita in order to be able to be next to the Girl with the Golden Eyes when they turned back, Paquita, no less impatient, quickly came forward, and de Marsay felt his hand pressed by her in a way that was both so quick and so passionately significant that he thought he had received the shock of an electric spark. In an instant all the emotions of his youth welled up in his heart. When the two lovers looked at each other, Paquita seemed ashamed; she lowered her eyes so as not to see Henri's again, but her gaze slipped down to look at the feet and figure of the one whom women before the revolution used to call 'their conqueror.'

"I will definitely have this woman as my mistress," Henri said to himself.

Following her to the end of the terrace, on the edge of the Place Louis-XV, he saw the old

Marquis de San-Réal who was advancing, propped on the arm of his valet, walking with all the precaution of a gouty, doddering old man. Doña Concha, who mistrusted Henri, made Paquita go between her and the old man.

"Oh! You," de Marsay said to himself, aiming a scornful look at the duenna, "if we can't make you give in, with a little opium we'll put you to sleep. We know our mythology, and the fable of Argus."

Before she climbed into the carriage, the Girl with the Golden Eyes exchanged some glances with her lover about whose meaning there could be no doubt, and which delighted Henri; but the duenna caught one of them, and spoke some words brusquely to Paquita, who threw herself into the carriage with a despairing air. For some days Paquita didn't come to the Tuileries. Laurent, who, by order of his master, went to keep watch by her mansion, learned from the neighbors that neither the two women nor the old Marquis had gone out since the day when the duenna had surprised a look between the young lady under her guard and Henri. The link that united the two lovers, so weak, was already broken, then.

A few days later, without anyone knowing how, de Marsay had succeeded at his plan: He had a seal and some wax that were completely similar to the seal and wax that sealed the letters sent from

London to Mlle. Valdès, paper similar to the kind the correspondent used, and all the utensils and blocking stamps necessary to put English and French stamps and postmarks on it. He had written the following letter, upon which he set all the marks of a letter sent from London.

Dear Paquita, I will not attempt to portray for you, in words, the passion you have inspired in me. If, to my great joy, you share it, know that I have found the means to correspond with you. My name is Adolphe de Gouges, and I live on the Rue de l'Université, No. 54. If you are too well-guarded to write to me, if you have no paper or pens, I will know by your silence. Therefore, if tomorrow, from eight in the morning till ten at night, you haven't thrown a letter over the wall of your garden into that of the Baron de Nucingen, where someone will wait all day, a man who is completely devoted to me will slip over the wall to you, attached to a rope, two flasks, at ten in the morning the next day—be sure to go out for a stroll around that time. One of the flasks will contain opium to put your Argus to sleep, you just need to give her six drops. The other will contain ink. The ink flask is cut-glass, the other is plain.

Both are flat enough for you to be able to hide them in your bodice. All that I've done already to be able to correspond with you must tell you how much I love you. If you doubt me, I swear to you that, to obtain an hour's meeting with you, I would give my life.

"They actually believe that, the poor creatures!" de Marsay said to himself; "but they are right to. What would we think of a woman who wouldn't let herself be seduced by a love letter accompanied by such convincing circumstances?"

This letter was delivered by Master Moinot, the mailman, the next day, around eight in the morning, to the concierge of the San-Réal mansion.

To get closer to the battlefield, de Marsay had come to lunch at Paul's house, on the Rue de la Pépinière. At two o'clock, when the two friends were laughingly regaling each other with the discomfiture of a young man who had wanted to live elegantly without any well-established wealth, and as they were trying to think of a good end to the story, Henri's coachman came looking for his master at Paul's, and presented him with a mysterious individual who wanted urgently to speak with him. This character was a mulatto from whom Talma, the great actor, could certainly have drawn inspiration to play Othello, if he had met him. Never did an African face more eloquently express grandeur in vengeance, rapidity of suspicion, promptitude in the execution of a thought, the strength of the Moor and his childish impulsiveness. His black eyes had the fixed look of the eyes of a bird of prey, and they were set, like a vulture's, beneath a dusky membrane void of eyelashes. There was something menacing about his small, low forehead. Obviously this man was under the yoke of one single thought. The sinews of his arm didn't belong to him. He was followed in by a man that any sort of consciousness, whether of those shivering in Greenland or those sweating in New England, would describe with this phrase: *He was an unhappy man.* With this phrase, anyone can imagine his appearance, can represent him for themselves according to the ideas particular to each country. But who can imagine his pale, wrinkled face, reddened at nose and ears, and his long beard? Who can see his yellowish whipcord cravat, his thick collar, his battered hat, his greenish frock coat, his pitiful trousers, his shriveled waistcoat, his fake gold tiepin, his muddy shoes, the laces of which had been mired in muck? Who will understand him in all the immensity of his present and past misery? Who? Only the Parisian. The unhappy man of Paris is the complete unhappy man, for he encounters enough joy to know just how unhappy he is. The mulatto seemed to be an executioner under Louis XI leading a man to be hanged.

"Who has fished up these two characters for us?" Henri asked.

"Good Lord! One of them really gives me the shivers," Paul replied.

"You—the one who looks most Christian of you two—who are you?" Henri said, looking at the unhappy man.

The mulatto stayed with his eyes fixed on these two young men, like a man who heard nothing, but who was still trying to guess something from gestures and lip movements.

"I am a public letter-writer and an interpreter. I live by the Law Courts, and my name is Poincet."

"Fine! And that one?" Henri said to Poincet, pointing at the mulatto.

"I don't know; he only speaks a kind of Spanish dialect, and he brought me here to be able to communicate with you."

The mulatto took out of his pocket the letter Henri had written to Paquita, and gave it to Henri, who threw it in the fire.

"Well, now something's starting to take shape," Henri said to himself. "Paul, leave us alone for a moment."

"I translated this letter for him, the interpreter continued when they were alone. "When it was translated, he went somewhere, I don't know where. Then he came back looking for me, to bring me here, promising me two louis."

"What do you have to say to me, Chinaman?" Henri asked.

"I didn't mention the Chinese part," the interpreter said as he waited for the mulatto's reply.

"He says, Monsieur," the interpreter continued after listening to the unknown man, "that you have to be on Boulevard Montmartre, near the café, at 10:30 tomorrow night. You'll see a carriage there, which you will climb into, saying to the one who will be ready to open the door the password *cortejo*—a Spanish word that means *lover*," Poincet added, directing a congratulatory look at Henri.

"Very well!"

The mulatto wanted to give Poincet two louis; but de Marsay wouldn't allow this and paid the interpreter himself; as he was paying him, the mulatto said something.

"What is he saying?"

"He is warning me," the unhappy man replied, "that, if I commit one single indiscretion, he will strangle me. He looks kind enough, and he looks quite capable of doing so."

"I'm sure he is," Henri replied. "He would do just what he says."

"He adds," the interpreter continued, "that the person whose messenger he is begs you, for you and for her, to act with the greatest prudence, because the daggers raised over your heads would

67

THE GIRL WITH THE GOLDEN EYES

fall into your hearts, and no human agency could save you from them."

"He said that! All the better, it will be more amusing. –You can come back in, Paul!" he shouted to his friend.

The mulatto, who hadn't stopped looking at Paquita Valdès' lover with magnetic attention, went out, followed by the interpreter.

"Finally, here is a truly romantic adventure," Henri said to himself when Paul returned. "After taking part in a few, I've finally encountered in this Paris of ours an intrigue accompanied by dangerous circumstances, major perils. By Jove, how bold danger makes woman! To annoy a woman, to try to constrain her, doesn't that give her the right and the courage to leap barriers in an instant that she would have taken years to climb over? Sweet creature, go on, jump! Die? Poor child! Daggers? The fancies of women! They all feel the need to give gravity to their little escapade. But we'll keep them in mind, Paquita! We'll keep them in mind, my girl! Devil take me, now that I know that this beautiful girl, this masterpiece of nature, is mine, the adventure has lost its edge."

Despite this flippant speech, the boy had resurfaced in Henri. To wait till the next day without suffering, he had recourse to exorbitant pleasures: He gambled, dined, supped with his friends; he drank like a coachman, ate like a German, and won ten or twelve thousand francs. At two in the morning he left the Rocher de Cancale, slept like a child, woke up the next day fresh and pink, and got dressed to go to the Tuileries, deciding to go riding on horseback after seeing Paquita so as to work up an appetite and dine better, in order to be able to pass the time more quickly.

At the appointed hour, Henri was on the boulevard, saw the carriage, and gave the password to a man who looked to him like the mulatto. When he heard this word, the man opened the door and quickly unfolded the step. Henri was carried so rapidly through Paris, and his thoughts left him with so little ability to pay attention to the streets through which they were passing, that he didn't notice where the carriage stopped. The mulatto led him into a house where the steps were close to the carriage entrance. This stairway was dark, as was the landing, on which Henri was obliged to wait while the mulatto set about opening the door of a dank, foul-smelling apartment with no light, the rooms of which, barely illumined by the candle his guide found in the antechamber, seemed to him empty and sparsely furnished, like the rooms of a house whose inhabitants are away traveling. He recognized that sensation he got when he read one of those novels by Ann Radcliffe where the hero passes through the cold, dark, uninhabited rooms of some sad and deserted place. Finally the mulatto opened the door of a drawing room. The condition of the old furniture and faded draperies with which this room was decorated made it resemble the salon of a bordello. Here there was the same pretension to elegance and the same assemblage of things in poor taste, the dust, the grime. On a sofa covered in velvet of Utrecht red, in the corner of a smoking hearth, whose fire was buried in ashes, a poorly dressed old woman was sitting, wearing one of those turbans that English women know how to devise when they reach a certain age, and which would meet with an infinite success in China, where the ideal beauty of artists is monstrosity. This salon, this old woman, this cold hearth, all this would have chilled his love, if Paquita herself had not been there, on a love seat, in a voluptuous dressing gown, free to aim her glances of gold and flame, free to show her curved foot, free with her luminous movements. This first interview was like all first encounters that passionate people grant each other: They have rapidly traveled long distances, and desire each other ardently, but they don't know each other yet. It is impossible for there not to be some disharmony at first in this situation, bothersome only till the moment when their souls have found the same level. If desire makes a man bold and inclines him not to plan anything, so as not to seem feminine, the mistress, however extreme her love is, is terrified at finding herself so quickly reaching her goal, face to face with the necessity of giving herself, which for many women is like falling into an abyss and not knowing what they'll find at the bottom. The involuntary coldness of this woman contrasts with her avowed passion, and necessarily reacts on even the most smitten lover. These ideas, which often float like vapors around souls, establish a kind of transient sickness there. In the sweet journey that two people undertake through the beautiful countries of love, this moment is like a moorland to cross, a moor without heather, humid and hot by turns, or full of burning sands, cut off by swamps, leading to joyous groves clothed in roses where love and its processions of pleasures unfurl onto carpets of fine greensward. Often a witty man finds himself endowed with an idiotic laugh that serves as his reply to everything; his mind is dulled beneath the glacial compression of his desires. It would not be impossible for two equally handsome, spiritual, and passionate beings to start out by saying the most idiotic commonplaces, until chance, a word, the trembling of a certain look, the communication of an electric spark, makes them come to the happy transition that leads them onto the flowery path where you don't walk, but where you glide along without ever descending. This state of the soul always comes from the very violence of the emotions. Two beings who love each other feebly experience nothing like it. The effect of this crisis can also be compared to the effect produced by the glare of an unclouded sky. At first glance nature seems to be covered with gauze, the azure of the firmament looks black, extreme light looks like darkness. In Henri, as well as in the Spanish girl, a similar violence was present; and that law of physics by virtue of which two identical forces cancel each other out when they meet could also be true in the moral realm. Furthermore, the embarrassment of this moment was notably increased by the presence of the old mummy.

Love can be frightened or stimulated by anything. To it, everything has meaning, everything is a happy or foreboding omen. This decrepit woman was there as a possible outcome, and represented the horrid fish tail with which the geniuses of symbolism in Ancient Greece equipped the Chimeras and the Sirens, so seductive, so deceptive from the waist up, as all passions are in the beginning. Henri, though not a hardy spirit—that phrase is always mocking—but a man of extraordinary power, a man as great as you can be without belief, was struck by the totality of all these circumstances.

Moreover the strongest men are naturally the most impressionable, and consequently the most superstitious, if you can still call "superstition" the prejudice of the first impulse, which no doubt is actually insight into the results of causes hidden from other eyes, but perceptible to their own.

The Spanish girl took advantage of this moment of astonishment to succumb to that ecstasy of infinite adoration that seizes a woman's heart when she truly loves someone, and when she finds herself in the presence of a vainly desired idol. Her eyes were full of joy and happiness, and gleams of light came from them. She was under his spell, and was intoxicated by a long dreamed-of bliss, without fear. She seemed wonderfully beautiful then to Henri, so that all this phantasmagoria of tattered cloth, decay, frayed red draperies, green mats before the armchairs, worn red tile floor—all this distressed, diseased luxury—immediately disappeared. The drawing room was lit up; he could see the terrible, motionless harpy, silent on her red sofa, only through a cloud. Her yellow eyes betrayed the servile emotions aroused by misfortune or caused by a vice under whose slavery one has fallen, as if under a tyrant who exhausts you beneath the flagellations of his despotism. Her eyes had the cold brilliance of the eyes of a caged tiger aware of its powerlessness, who finds it is forced to devour its own destructive desires.

"Who is this woman?" Henri asked Paquita.

But Paquita didn't reply. She made a sign that she didn't understand French, and asked Henri if he spoke English. De Marsay repeated his question in English.

"She is the only woman I can trust, even though she has already sold me," Paquita said calmly. "My dear Adolphe, she is my mother, a slave bought in Georgia for her rare beauty, hardly any of which remains today. She speaks nothing but her mother tongue."

The attitude of this woman, and her wish to divine what was going on between her daughter and Henri from their movements, were suddenly explained to the young man, and put him more at ease.

"Paquita," he said to her, "we won't ever be free, then?"

"Never!" she said sadly. "Even now we don't have many days left us."

She lowered her eyes, looked at her hand, and with her right hand counted the fingers on her left hand, thus displaying the most beautiful hands Henri had ever seen.

"One, two, three…"

She counted up to twelve.

"Yes," she said, "we have twelve days left."

"And then?"

"Then," she said, remaining as self-absorbed as a frail woman before the executioner's axe, as if killed beforehand by a fear that stripped her of that magnificent energy that nature seemed to have granted only to increase sensual delights and convert the coarsest pleasures into endless poetry. "Then," she repeated. Her eyes became fixed; she seemed to contemplate a distant, threatening object. "I don't know," she said.

"This girl is mad," Henri said to himself, and thereupon fell into a strange reverie.

Paquita seemed to him preoccupied by something other than himself; she was like a woman under the influence of both remorse and passion. Maybe she had another love in her heart that she alternately forgot and remembered. In an instant, Henri was assailed by a thousand contradictory thoughts. This girl became a mystery to him; but, contemplating her with the expert attention of the world-weary, a man starved for new sensual pleasures, like that Oriental monarch who asked for a new pleasure to be created for him—a horrible thirst to which great souls are prey—Henri recognized in Paquita the richest combination nature has ever created for love. The presumed workings of this mechanism, with its soul set aside, would have frightened any other man but de Marsay; but he was fascinated by this wealth of promised pleasures, by this constant variety in happiness, every man's dream, and also what every woman in love strives for. He was driven wild by the infinite made palpable, and transported into the creature's most excessive delights. He saw all that in this girl more clearly than he had ever yet seen it, for she complacently let herself be observed, glad to be admired. De Marsay's admiration became a secret rage, and he revealed it completely in the looks he gave the Spanish girl that she understood, as if she were used to receiving such looks.

"If you were not going to be mine alone, I would kill you!" he cried out.

Hearing this, Paquita covered her face with her hands and naively cried: "Holy Virgin, what have I gotten myself into?"

She got up, threw herself on the red sofa, plunged her head into the rags that covered her mother's bosom, and wept. The old lady received her daughter without emerging from her immobility, without showing her any emotion. The mother exhibited to the fullest that gravity of savage peoples, that impassivity of statues, on which observation runs aground. Did she, or did she not, love her daughter? No answer. Beneath this mask all human emotions were smoldering, good and bad, and anything at all might be expected from this creature. Her gaze passed slowly from her daughter's beautiful hair, which covered her like a mantle, to Henri's face, which she observed with an inexpressible curiosity. She seemed to be wondering by what magic spell he was there, by what caprice nature had made so seductive a man.

"These women are making fun of me!" Henri said to himself.

At that instant, Paquita raised her head and gave him one of those looks that sear your soul and burn you. She looked so beautiful to him that he swore to himself he would possess this treasure of beauty.

"My Paquita, be mine!"

"Do you want to kill me?" she said, fearful, trembling, anxious, but led back to him by some inexplicable force.

"Me, kill you!" he said, smiling.

Paquita let out a cry of fear and said a word to the old woman, who took Henri's hand without asking, and her daughter's hand, studied them a long time, then returned their hands to them, nodding her head in a horribly significant way.

"Be mine tonight, this very instant, follow me, don't leave me, you must, Paquita! Do you love me? Come with me!"

In an instant, he said a thousand senseless words to her with the rapidity of a torrent leaping between rocks, repeating the same sound in a thousand different ways.

"It's the same voice!" Paquita said sadly, without de Marsay hearing her, "and... the same fervor," she added.

"All right, yes," she said with an abandon of passion that nothing could express. "Yes, but not tonight. Tonight, Adolphe, I didn't give enough opium to the *Concha*, she might wake up, I would be lost. At this moment, everyone in the house thinks I'm asleep in my bedroom. In two days, be at the same spot, say the same word to the same man. This man is my foster father, Christemio adores me and would die in torment for me without anyone being able to tear a word against me from him. Adieu," she said, seizing Henri's body and twisting herself around him like a snake.

She squeezed him tight, brought her head up to his, offered her lips, and gave him a kiss that gave them both such vertigo that de Marsay thought the earth was opening up, and then Paquita cried out, "Go away!" in a voice that let him know how little in control of herself she really was. But she clung to him, still crying "Go!", and led him slowly to the stairway.

There the mulatto, whose white eyes lit up at sight of Paquita, took the torch from his idol's hands, and led Henri out to the street. He left the torch under the archway, opened the door, put Henri back in the carriage, and let him out on the

Boulevard des Italiens with amazing speed. The horses seemed to have hellfire in their bodies.

The scene was like a dream for de Marsay, but one of those dreams that, even as they evaporate, leave behind a feeling of supernatural voluptuousness in the soul, which a man chases after for the rest of his life. One single kiss had been enough. No tryst had ever taken place in so decent a way, or so chaste, or even so cold, in a place made more terrible in its details, before a more hideous divinity—for this mother of hers had stayed in Henri's imagination like something hellish, crouching, cadaverous, vicious, savage, something the fantasies of painters and poets had not yet guessed. In actual fact, never had a tryst more inflamed his senses, or revealed to him bolder sensual delights, or made love gush more from his core to spread itself like an atmosphere around a man. This was something dark, mysterious, sweet, tender, constrained and expansive, a pairing of the horrible and the heavenly, of paradise and hell, that made de Marsay almost drunk. He was no longer himself, and yet he was old enough to be able to resist the intoxications of pleasure.

In order to understand de Marsay's behavior at the end of this story, it must be explained how his soul had expanded at an age when most young men's shrank from getting mixed up with women or having too much to do with them. His soul had grown through a combination of secret circumstances that endowed him with an immense unknown power. This young man held a scepter in his hand that was more powerful than that of modern kings, almost all of them restrained by laws in even their slightest wishes. De Marsay wielded the autocratic power of the Oriental despot. But this power, so stupidly put into practice in Asia by coarse men, was increased tenfold by European intelligence and by French wit—the liveliest, keenest of all instruments of the mind. Henri could do whatever he liked in the interest of his pleasures and his vanities. This invisible action on the social world had clothed him in a real but secret majesty, discreet, folded in on itself. He had about himself, not the opinion that Louis XIV would have had, but what the proudest of Caliphs, of Pharaohs, of Xerxes who believe they belong to the divine race, had about themselves, when they imitated God by veiling themselves from their subjects, under the pretext that their gaze caused death. Thus, without having any remorse at being both judge and plaintiff, de Marsay coldly condemned to death the man or woman who had seriously offended him. Although often pronounced almost offhandedly, the sentence was irrevocable. A mere foible became a catastrophe, like lightning striking some happy Parisian girl in her fiacre, instead of killing the old coachman who is bringing her to a tryst. Thus the bitter, profound pleasantry that marked the conversation of this young man generally caused fear in others; no one felt a desire to challenge him. Women intensely love those who call themselves "pashas," who seem as if they're accompanied by lions and executioners, and who walk clothed in terror. These men have an ensuing confidence of action, a certainty of power, a pride of look, a leonine awareness that for women embody the type of strength they all dream of. De Marsay was such a man.

Joyous at that instant with his future, he became once again young and vibrant, and thought only of love as he went to bed. He dreamed of the Girl with the Golden Eyes, as passionate young men dream: monstrous images, elusive peculiarities, full of light, which reveal invisible worlds, but always in an incomplete way, for the interposing veil changes optic conditions. The next day and the day after that, he disappeared without anyone knowing where he had gone. His power belonged to him only on certain conditions, and fortunately for him, during these two days, he was a simple soldier in the service of the demon whose talismanic existence he possessed. But at the agreed-upon time, that night, on the boulevard, he waited for the carriage, which wasn't late in coming. The mulatto approached Henri to tell him, in French, a phrase he seemed to have learned by heart: "If you want to come, she told me, you have to agree to have your eyes blindfolded."

And Christemio showed him a scarf of white silk.

"No!" Henri said, whose omnipotence suddenly rebelled.

And he wanted to climb in. The mulatto gave a sign; the carriage started off.

"Yes!" de Marsay cried, furious at losing a happiness that had been promised him. Moreover, he saw the impossibility of arguing with a slave whose obedience was blind as an executioner's. And why should it be on this passive instrument that his anger should fall?

The mulatto whistled; the carriage returned. Henri quickly climbed in. Already some curious onlookers were stupidly gathering on the boulevard. Henri was strong, he wanted to trick the mulatto. When the carriage left at a fast trot, he grabbed his hands, trying to get control of him so as, by overcoming his guard, to be able to keep the exercise of his faculties so he could know where he was going. Vain attempt. The mulatto's eyes gleamed in the shadows. The man uttered furious cries, got free, threw de Marsay down with an iron hand, and nailed him, so to speak, to the floor of the carriage. Then, with his free hand, he drew out a triangular dagger, and whistled. The coachman heard the whistle, and stopped. Henri, weaponless, was forced to give in; he offered his head for the blindfold. This gesture of submission appeased Christemio, who tied his eyes with a respect and care that testified to a kind of veneration for the body of the man his idol loved. But, before taking this precaution, he had defiantly put his dagger away in his side pocket, and buttoned himself up to his chin.

"He would have killed me, that Chinaman!" de Marsay said to himself.

The carriage quickly started up again. One resource remained for a young man who knew Paris as well as Henri knew it. To learn where he was going, it was enough for him to concentrate and count, by the number of gutters they crossed, the streets they passed on the boulevards, as long as the carriage continued to go straight ahead. He could thus recognize along which side street the carriage would head, whether towards the Seine, or towards the hills of Montmartre, and guess the name or position of the street where his guide would stop. But the violent emotion that his struggle had caused him, the fury at his compromised dignity, the ideas of revenge he dwelt on, the suppositions suggested to him by the meticulous care this mysterious girl was taking to bring him to her—all this prevented him from having that blind man's attention necessary to the concentration of his intelligence and to the perfect hindsight of memory. The journey lasted half an hour. When the carriage stopped, it was no longer on a paved road. The mulatto and the coachman took Henri bodily round the waist, lifted him up, put him on a kind of stretcher, and carried him through a garden whose flowers and particular odor of the trees and greenery Henri could smell. The silence that reigned there was so profound that he could make out the sound a few drops of water made as they fell from wet leaves. The two men carried him into a stairway, made him stand up, then led him through several rooms, guiding him by the hands, and left him in a room whose atmosphere was perfumed, and whose thick rug he could feel beneath his feet. A woman's hand pushed him onto a divan and untied his blindfold. Henri saw Paquita in front of him, but Paquita in her glory as a voluptuous woman.

One half of the boudoir in which Henri found himself described a softly gracious circular outline, which contrasted with the other part perfectly square, in the middle of which gleamed a mantelpiece of white marble and gold. He had entered by a side door concealed beneath a rich tapestry curtain, which faced a window. The horseshoe part of the chamber was adorned with a real Turkish divan, that is to say a mattress placed on the ground, but a mattress deep as a bed, a divan fifty feet around, in white cashmere, adorned by black and poppy-red silk tassels arranged in diamond patterns. The back of this immense bed rose several inches above the many cushions that enriched it even more by their tasteful charm. This boudoir was hung with a red fabric overlaid by the sheerest Indian chiffon, fluted like a Corinthian column, its folds alternately hollow and full, ending at both top and bottom in a poppy red band of cloth on which black arabesques were outlined. Beneath the sheer muslin, the red cloth showed as pink, an amorous color that was repeated by the curtains on the window, made of Indian chiffon lined with pink taffeta, and adorned with poppy-red fringes mixed with black. Six silver gilt sconces, each supporting two candles, were attached to the wall-hangings at equal distances to illumine the divan. The ceiling, in the center of which hung a burnished silver chandelier, gleamed white, and the cornice was gilt. The rug was like a shawl from the Orient; it represented the pictures and recalled the poems of Persia, where the hands of slaves had labored on it. All the furniture was covered in white cashmere, enhanced by black and poppy-red accents. The clock, the candelabra, everything was white marble and gold. The solitary table had a cashmere shawl as covering. Elegant flower arrangements contained all kinds of roses, along with white or red flowers. The slightest detail seemed in fact to have been the object of the most loving attention. Never was richness more coquettishly veiled to become elegance, to express grace, to inspire voluptuousness. Here everything would have warmed the heart of even the coldest being. The way the hangings shimmered, their color always changing according to the direction of your gaze, becoming either completely white, or completely pink, harmonized with the effects of the light infused in the diaphanous folds of chiffon, producing a misty appearance. The soul has some sort of attachment to white; love is pleased by red; and gold flatters the passions, and has the power to realize their fantasies. Thus whatever vague and mysterious qualities there are in man, all his unexplained affinities, were caressed through their involuntary resemblances. There was a concert of colors in this perfect harmony to which the soul responded with voluptuous, indecisive, floating ideas.

It was in the midst of this hazy atmosphere charged with exquisite perfumes that Paquita, wearing a white dressing gown, her feet bare, orange blossoms in her black hair, appeared kneeling before Henri, adoring him like the god of this temple he had deigned to visit. Although de Marsay was accustomed to seeing the affectations of Parisian luxury, he was surprised at the appearance of this shell, so like the one from which Venus was born. Either because of the contrast between the darkness from which he had emerged and the light flooding his soul, or from a quick comparison between this scene and that of the first meeting, he experienced one of those delicate sensations that true poetry produces. When he caught sight, in the middle of this sanctum appearing from a fairy's wand, of that masterpiece of creation, this girl, whose warmly suffused complexion, whose soft skin lightly gilded by the reflections of red and by the effusion of some unknown vapor of love, glowed as if she were reflecting the beams of lights and colors, then all his anger, his desires for revenge, his wounded vanity, fell away from him. Like an eagle swooping down on his prey, he seized her round the waist, seated her on his lap, and with an inexpressible drunkenness felt the voluptuous pressure of this girl whose charms, so generously developed, gently enveloped him.

"Come, Paquita!" he said in a low voice.

"Speak! Speak without fear," she said to him. "This retreat was built for love. No sound can escape it, designed as it is with the aim of cherishing the accents and musical tones of the beloved's voice. However loud our cries here, they cannot be heard beyond this enclosure. Someone could be killed here, but his moans would be as vain as if he were in the middle of the Great Desert."

"Who is it who has so well understood jealousy and its needs?"

"Never ask me about that," she replied, undoing the young man's cravat with an incredible tenderness, no doubt the better to see his neck.

"Yes, there is the neck I love so well!" she said. "Do you want to please me?"

This question, almost lascivious in its tone, raised de Marsay out of the reverie into which he had been plunged by the despotic reply with which Paquita had forbidden him any research into the unknown being who was floating like a shade above them.

"And what if I wanted to know who rules here?"

Paquita looked at him, trembling.

"It isn't me, then," he said, standing up and ridding himself of the girl, who fell head backwards. "I want to be the only one, wherever I am."

"Just like! Just like!" the poor slave cried, prey to terror.

"Who do you take me for, then? Will you answer?"

Paquita slowly got up, her eyes full of tears, went over to one of the two ebony cupboards and took out a dagger, which she held out to Henri with a gesture of submission that would have softened a tiger.

"Give me a feast such as only people who love each other can give," she said, "and then when I am asleep, kill me, for I cannot answer you.

Listen: I am bound like a poor animal to its stake; I am astonished that I've been able to throw a bridge over the abyss that separates us. Make me drunk, then kill me. Oh! No, no," she said clasping her hands, "don't kill me! I love life! Life is so beautiful to me! If I am a slave, I am a queen too. I could deceive you with words, tell you I love no one but you, prove it to you, take advantage of my momentary power to say to you: 'Take me the way one tastes in passing the perfume of a flower in the garden of a king.' Then, after using the clever eloquence of woman and the wings of pleasure, after quenching my thirst, I could have you thrown into a pit where no one would find you, one which was constructed to satisfy revenge without having to fear that of justice, a pit full of quicklime that would burn you and consume you without a morsel of your body ever being found. You would remain in my heart, mine forever."

Henri looked at this girl without trembling, and his fearless gaze overwhelmed her with joy.

"No, I won't do it! You haven't fallen into a trap here, but into the heart of a woman who adores you, and I am the one who will be thrown into the pit."

"All that seems immensely strange to me," de Marsay said as he gazed at her. "But you seem a good girl to me, though one with a strange nature; you are, upon my word, a living riddle, the answer to which seems to me difficult to find indeed."

Paquita understood none of what the young man was saying; she looked at him gently, opening eyes that could never be dull, so much voluptuousness was portrayed there.

"Listen, my love," she said, returning to her first idea, "do you want to please me?"

"I will do whatever you like, and even some things that you don't," de Marsay replied laughing, resuming his usual conceited nonchalance and resolving to let himself be led by this affair without looking back or forward. And he might also have been counting on his power, and on the adroitness of a man favored by fortune, to dominate this girl a few hours later, and learn all her secrets.

"Well," she said, "let me arrange you to my taste."

"Make me look however you like, then," Henri said.

Delighted, Paquita went over to one of the two wardrobes and took out a red velvet dress, in which she dressed de Marsay; then she put a woman's hat on him and wrapped him in a shawl. As she gave herself up to these mad fancies, performed with a child's innocence, she laughed convulsively, and looked like a bird beating her wings; but she saw nothing beyond the present.

If it is impossible to portray the extraordinary delights that these two handsome creatures, fashioned by heaven one time when it was full of joy, experienced, it might perhaps be necessary to convey metaphysically the extraordinary, almost fantastic impressions of the young man. What people who find themselves in the social situation de Marsay occupied, and who live as he lived, can recognize best, is the innocence of a girl. But, strange thing! If the Girl with the Golden Eyes was a virgin, she was certainly not innocent. The strange union of the mysterious and the actual, shadow and light, the horrible and the beautiful, pleasure and danger, Paradise and Hell, which had already been encountered in this adventure, was sustained by this capricious, sublime being de Marsay was enjoying. The most knowing and most refined voluptuousness—whatever Henri could comprehend of that poetry of the senses they call 'love'—was surpassed by the treasures that poured from this girl whose brimming eyes didn't lie about any of the promises they made. It was an Oriental poem where the sun shone that Saadi, or Hafiz, put into their vivacious verses. But neither Saadi's rhythm nor Pindar's could have expressed the ecstasy full of confusion and intoxication with which this delicious girl was seized when the illusion dissolved in which an iron hand had been compelling her to live.

"Dead!" she said, "I am dead! Adolphe, take me away to the ends of the earth, to an island where no one knows us. Make sure our flight leaves no traces! We would be followed down into Hell. Oh God! The day is dawning. Save yourself. Will I ever see you again? Yes, tomorrow, I want to see you again, even if, to have that happiness, I had to put all my guardians to death. Till tomorrow."

She clasped him in her arms in an embrace that was full of the terror of death. Then she touched a spring that must have been attached to a bell, and begged de Marsay to let himself be blindfolded.

"What if I refused, what if I wanted to stay here?"

"You would cause my death more quickly," she said; "for now I am sure I will die for you."

Henri let himself be blindfolded. There sometimes occurs in a man who has just feasted on pleasure a slope into oblivion, a strange kind of ingratitude, a desire for freedom, a wish just to go outside for a walk, a tinge of scorn and perhaps disgust for his idol—inexplicable sentiments arise that render him loathsome and base. The certainty of this confused but real emotion in souls that are neither enlightened by that heavenly light nor perfumed by that holy balm whence pertinacity of sentiment comes to us, no doubt dictated to Rousseau the adventures of Milord Édouard with which the letters of *La Nouvelle Héloïse* conclude. (If Rousseau was obviously inspired by the work of Richardson, he strayed from it in a thousand details that leave his monument magnificently original;

he has commended it to posterity by great ideas difficult to explicate by analysis, when, in one's youth, one reads this work with the aim of finding in it the warm portrayal of the most physical of our emotions, while serious writers and philosophers never use its images except as the consequence or necessity of profound thought; and the adventures of Milord Édouard are one of the most European, delicate ideas in this work.)

Henri found himself, then, under the power of this confused feeling that true love does not experience. For Henri to be drawn back to a woman, the persuasive power of comparisons had to cease, while the attractions of memories had somehow to exert their irresistible influence. True love rules, above all, through memory. Can the woman who has not been engraved in the soul by either excess of pleasure or force of feeling ever be loved? Without Henri's being aware of it, Paquita had become established in him by these two means. But at this moment, wholly absorbed by the fatigue of happiness, that delicious melancholy of the body, he could hardly analyze his heart by trying again on his lips the taste of the liveliest sensual delights he had ever plucked. He found himself on the Boulevard Montmartre at daybreak, stupidly watched the departing carriage, took two cigars out of his pocket, lit one from the lamp of a woman who sold brandy and coffee to workmen, children, market farmers—to all the Parisian population that starts its life before daybreak. Then he went his way, smoking his cigar, shoving his hands in his pants pockets with a truly dishonorable insouciance.

"What a good thing a cigar is! Here's something a man will never tire of," he said to himself.

He scarcely thought of that Girl with the Golden Eyes who was all the rage then among the elegant young men of Paris. The idea of death that ran through their pleasures, the fear of death that had several times darkened the brow of that beautiful creature who was linked to the houris of Asia by her mother, to Europe by her education, to the Tropics by her birth, seemed to him one of those ruses by which all women try to make themselves interesting.

"She is from Havana, from the most Spanish country there is in the New World; so she preferred to play on themes of terror rather than throw in my face suffering and arduousness, coquetry or duty, as Parisian ladies do. By those golden eyes of hers, I'd love to get some sleep!"

He saw a cabriolet stationed on the corner of Frascati's, waiting for some gamblers; he woke the coachman up, had him drive him home, went to bed, and slept the sleep of bad citizens, which, by an odd coincidence that no songwriter has yet turned to his advantage, also happens to be as profound as the sleep of innocence. Perhaps this is an effect of that proverbial axiom, *extremes meet.*

Around noon de Marsay stretched his arms as he woke up, and felt the attacks of one of those bouts of canine hunger that all old soldiers can remember experiencing the day after victory. In front of him he saw Paul de Manerville; he was happy at this, for there is nothing more agreeable than eating in company.

"So here you are," his friend said to him, "we were all imagining that you had locked yourself up for ten days with the Girl with the Golden Eyes."

"The Girl with the Golden Eyes! I don't think about her anymore. I have lots of other fish to fry."

"Oh! You're the soul of discretion."

"Why not?" de Marsay said, laughing. "My dear man, discretion is the cleverest kind of self-interest. Listen.... No, I won't breathe a word to you. You never teach me anything, so I'm not inclined to give away the treasures of my policies, getting nothing in return. Life is a river that serves to create business. By all that is most sacred on Earth, by cigars, I'm not a professor of social economy at the service of simpletons. Let's have lunch. It costs less to give you a tuna omelet than to pour out my brain to you."

"You keep tabs with your friends?"

"My dear man," said Henri, who could rarely pass up an ironic statement, "since you're just as likely as anyone else to have need of discretion someday, and since I like you very much.... Yes, I like you! My word of honor, if all that was necessary to keep you from blowing your brains out was a thousand-franc note, you'd find it here, since we haven't put that at risk yet, have we, Paul? If you were duelling tomorrow, I'd measure the distance and load the pistols, so that you'd be killed according to the rules. Finally, if anybody besides me dared to badmouth you in your absence, he'd have to stand up to the tough fellow he'd find in my skin— that's what I call a staunch friendship. Well then, when you need discretion, my little one, know that there exist two kinds: active discretion and negative discretion. Negative discretion is the kind idiots have—they use silence, negation, scowls, the discretion of closed doors, veritable impotence! Active discretion proceeds by affirmation. If tonight, at the club, I said, 'Dammit, the Girl with the Golden Eyes wasn't worth what she cost me!', everyone, after I left, would cry out: 'Did you hear that fop de Marsay try to get us to believe that he's already had the Girl with the Golden Eyes? He wanted to get rid of his rivals that way, the cunning man.' But that trick is vulgar, and dangerous. However coarse the stupid remark is that escapes us, there are always simpletons who might believe it. The best kind of discretion is the one that clever women use when they want to put their husbands off the track. It consists in compromising a woman to whom we are not attached, or whom we do not love, or whom we do not possess, to preserve the honor of the woman we love enough to respect her. That is what I call *the screen-woman.*—Aha! Here is Laurent. What are you bringing us?"

"Oysters from Ostend, Monsieur le Comte...."

"Someday you'll learn, Paul, how amusing it is to take people in by concealing from them the secret of our emotions. I feel immense pleasure in escaping the stupid jurisdiction of the masses, who never know what they want, or what they are made to want, who mistake the means for the result, who by turns adore and condemn, raise up and destroy! What happiness there is in imposing emotions on them and receiving none from them, of mastering them, never obeying them! If you can be proud of something, wouldn't that be of a power you yourself have acquired, for which we are at once the cause, the effect, the principle and the result? Well then, no one knows whom I love, or what I want. They might someday know whom I loved, what I would have liked, what I would have wanted, the way you know how a play ends; but would I ever let my hand be seen...? That would be weakness, or being duped. I know of nothing more despicable than force tricked by cunning. I am initiating myself, laughing all the way, into the role of ambassador, if diplomacy is as difficult as life, that is! I doubt it. Do you have any ambition? Do you want to become anything?"

"But, Henri, you're making fun of me, as if I weren't mediocre enough to succeed at everything."

"Very good, Paul! If you keep mocking yourself, you might soon be able to mock everyone else."

At lunch, after he had started smoking his cigars, de Marsay began to see the events of his night in a singular light. Like many great minds, his insight was not spontaneous; he didn't get to the bottom of things right away. As in all natures gifted with the faculty of living very much in the present, squeezing out its juice, so to speak, and devouring it, his second sight needed a kind of sleep before it could recognize causes. Cardinal de Richelieu was like that, who also did not lack the gift of foresight necessary for the conception of great things. De Marsay found himself with all these qualities, but he made use of his weapons only for the benefit of his pleasures, which are the first things a young man thinks of when he has gold and power. That is how a man becomes weathered: He uses women so that women cannot use him.

At that instant, then, de Marsay realized he had been tricked by the Girl with the Golden Eyes.

Now he saw in its entirety that night whose pleasures had only gradually started streaming forth, to end by pouring forth in torrents. Now he could read into this page so dazzling in its effect, and guess its hidden meaning. The purely physical innocence of Paquita, the astonishment of her joy, a few words that were obscure at first but clear now, that she let escape at the height of her pleasure—all this proved that he had actually stood in for someone else. Since none of the behavioral corruptions were unknown to him, since he professed complete indifference to all the caprices of desire, and thought them justified for the very reason that they could be satisfied, he was not shocked by vice. He knew vice as one knows a friend, but he was wounded at having served as food for it. If his presumptions were correct, he had been outraged in the living core of his being. The suspicion alone made him furious; he gave vent to the roar of a tiger mocked by a gazelle, the cry of a tiger that united a demonic intelligence with animal strength.

"What's wrong with you?" Paul asked him.

"Nothing!"

"I hope, if anyone ever asks you if you have anything against me, you wouldn't respond with a 'nothing' like that—we'd probably have to fight a duel the next day."

"I don't fight anymore," de Marsay said.

"That seems even more tragic. You assassinate, then?"

"You misuse words. I execute."

"My dear friend," Paul said, "your jokes are certainly dark, this morning."

"What would you expect? Sensuality leads to ferocity. Why? I don't know, and I'm not curious enough to find out why.—These cigars are excellent. Give your friend some tea.—Do you realize, Paul, that I lead the life of a brute? It's high time I chose a fate for myself, and used my strength for something worth the trouble of living. Life is a strange comedy. I am frightened; the inconsequence of our social order is ludicrous to me. The government has the heads chopped off poor devils who have killed one man, and it licenses creatures who, medically speaking, polish off a dozen young men every winter. Morality is powerless before a dozen vices that destroy society, and that nothing can punish. –Another cup?—My word of honor! Man is a buffoon dancing on a precipice. They preach to us about immorality in *Dangerous Liaisons*, and that other book with a housemaid's name for a title; but there exists a horrible, dirty, appalling, corrupt book, always open, which will never be closed: the great book of the world, not counting another book a thousand times more dangerous, which is composed of everything that is whispered into the ear, one man to another, or beneath a fan between women, at night, at a dance."

"Henri, there must be something extraordinary happening inside you; that's obvious, despite your active discretion."

"Yes! Listen, I have to eat up the time till tonight. Let's go play cards. Maybe I'll have the good fortune to lose."

De Marsay got up, took a handful of banknotes, rolled them up in his cigar case, got dressed, and used Paul's carriage to go to the Salon des Étrangers club, where he used up the time till evening in those moving alternatives of losing and winning that are the last resource of strong constitutions, when they are forced to exercise themselves in the void. When night came, he went to the meeting-place, and quietly let himself be blindfolded. Then, with that firm will to concentrate that only truly strong men have, he focused his attention and applied his intelligence to guessing what streets the carriage was traveling. He was almost certain he was being led to the Rue Saint-Lazare, and stopping at the little gate of the San-Réal garden. When he had gone through this gate, just as the first time, and was placed on a stretcher carried no doubt by the mulatto and the coachman, he understood, as he heard the sand crunch beneath their feet, why they were taking such careful precautions. If he had been unbound, or if he were walking, he could have plucked a branch from a shrub, studied the kind of sand stuck to his boots... whereas, transported so to speak through the air to an inaccessible mansion, his love affair went on being what it had been all along, a dream. But, to man's great despair, he can do nothing perfectly, either good or bad. All his intellectual or physical works are signed by a mark of destruction. It had rained a little; the ground was moist. During the night certain vegetable odors are much stronger than during the day; thus Henri could smell the fragrance of the mignonette flowers along the lane down which he was conveyed. This sign would enlighten him in the researches he promised himself he would carry out to recognize the mansion that held Paquita's boudoir. Likewise he paid close attention to the turns his bearers took in the house, and thought he could remember them. He saw he was on the ottoman like the night before, in front of Paquita who was undoing his scarf; but he saw she was pale and changed. She had been crying. Kneeling like an angel at prayer, but like a sad, profoundly melancholic angel, the poor girl no longer resembled the curious, urgent, leaping creature who had taken de Marsay on her wings to carry him up to the seventh heaven of love. There was something so real in this despair veiled by pleasure, that the terrible de Marsay felt in himself an admiration for this new masterpiece of nature, and temporarily forgot the main point of this meeting.

"What is wrong, my Paquita?"

"My friend," she said, "take me away, this very night! Cast me somewhere where they can't say when they see me: There is Paquita! where no one replies: Here is a girl with a golden gaze, who has long hair. In that place I will give you pleasures as long as you want them from me. Then, when you don't love me anymore, you can leave me, I won't complain, I won't say anything; and your abandoning me won't have to make you feel any remorse, since one day spent beside you, one single day during which I can look at you, will have been worth an entire life to me. But if I stay here, I am lost."

"I cannot leave Paris, my little one," Henri replied. "I am not my own master, I am tied by oath to the fate of many people who belong to me as I belong to them. But I can make a retreat for you in Paris, where no human power can reach."

"No," she said, "you forget feminine power."

Never had a phrase uttered by a human voice expressed terror more completely.

"What could reach you, then, if I place myself between you and the world?"

"Poison!" she said. "Already Doña Concha suspects you. And," she continued as tears streamed forth gleaming down her cheeks, "it is very easy to see that I am not the same anymore. Well, if you abandon me to the fury of the monster who will devour me, may your holy will be done!

But come, summon all the sensual delights of life to flourish in our love. In any case, I will beg, I will cry, I will shout, I will defend myself, I might even save myself."

"Who will you implore, then?" he said.

"Silence!" Paquita went on. "If I obtain my pardon, it might be because of my discretion."

"Give me my dress," Henri said insidiously.

"No, no," she replied spiritedly, "stay what you are, one of those angels I have been taught to hate, in whom I saw only monsters, whereas you are the handsomest thing under heaven," she said, caressing Henri's hair. "Don't you know what an idiot I am? I haven't learned anything. Since I was twelve years old, I've been shut up, without seeing anyone. I don't know how to read or write, I speak nothing but English and Spanish."

"How is it, then, that you receive letters from London?"

"My letters! Look, here they are!" she said, taking some papers out of a tall Japanese vase.

She held out to de Marsay some letters where the young man saw with surprise strange figures like those in a rebus, drawn with blood, which expressed phrases full of passion.

"But," he cried out, admiring these hieroglyphs created by a cunning jealousy, "are you under the power of an infernal genius?"

"Infernal," she repeated.

"But then how could you have gotten away..."

"Ha!" she said, "my doom stems from that. I placed Doña Concha between fear of immediate death and an anger to come. I had the curiosity of a demon, I wanted to break this bronze circle that had been drawn between the world and me, I wanted to see what young men are like, for the only men I know are the Marquis and Christemio. Our coachman and the valet who accompanies us are old men...."

"But, you weren't always locked up, were you? Your health..."

"Ha!" she continued, "we took walks, but only at night and in the countryside, by the Seine, far from other people."

"Aren't you proud of being so loved?"

"No," she said, "not any more! This hidden life, although full, is nothing but darkness compared with the light."

"What do you call 'light'?"

"You, my handsome Adolphe! You, for whom I would give my life. All the passionate things that I've been told and that I've inspired, I feel them all for you! Sometimes I understood nothing about existence, but now I know how we love. Till now I was loved, but I didn't love in return. I would leave everything for you—take me away! If you like, take me like a toy, but let me stay near you until you break me."

"You won't have any regrets?"

"Not one!" she said, letting him read her eyes, whose golden tint remained pure and clear.

"Am I her favorite?" Henri said to himself. Though he glimpsed the truth, he found himself in the position of forgiving the offense on account of so naïve a love. "I will see," he thought.

If Paquita didn't owe him any account of the past, the slightest memory became a crime to him. He had that regrettable strength of keeping his thoughts to himself, judging his mistress, studying her, while at the same time abandoning himself to the most stirring pleasures that a Peri fallen from paradise could ever have contrived for her beloved. Paquita seemed to have been created expressly by nature for love. From last night to this, her woman's genius had made the most rapid progress. What this young man's power was, and whatever his carefree attitude towards pleasure, despite his satiety the night before, he found in the Girl with the Golden Eyes that whole harem that a loving woman knows how to create, which a man never turns from. Paquita responded to the passion that all truly great men feel for the infinite, a mysterious passion so dramatically expressed in Faust, so poetically conveyed in Manfred, the one that drove Don Juan to sound the hearts of women, hoping to find there that limitless thought that so many ghost hunters go in search of, that learned men think they glimpse in science, and that mystics find in God alone. The hope that he had finally found the ideal Being with whom the struggle could be constant and tireless delighted de Marsay who, for the first time in a long time, opened up his heart to her. His nerves relaxed, his coldness melted in the atmosphere of this burning soul, his cold doctrines fled, and happiness colored his existence, like this white and pink boudoir. Sensing the stimulus of a superior voluptuousness, he was led beyond the limits within which he had till then enclosed his passion. He did not want to be surpassed by this girl who had been shaped to the needs of his soul in advance by a love that was in a sense artificial, so in that vanity of his that drives a man to be a conqueror in everything, he found the strength to dominate this girl; but also, hurled beyond that line where the soul is master of itself, he lost himself in that delicious limbo that common men so stupidly call *imaginary spaces*. He was tender, sweet, and communicative. He drove Paquita almost wild.

"Why shouldn't we go to Sorrento, to Nice, to Chiavari, to spend our lives this way? Would you like that?" he said to Paquita in a penetrating voice.

"Do you ever need to say 'Would you like that' to me?" she cried. "Do I have a will of my own? I am something outside of you only so that I can be a pleasure for you. If you want to choose a retreat worthy of us, Asia is the only country where love can spread its wings...."

"You are right," Henri said. "Let's go to the Indies, where Spring is eternal, where the earth is always full of flowers, where man can rule like a sovereign, without bumbling about as in these stupid countries where they want to realize the insipid pipe dreams of equality. Let's go to the country where you can live in the midst of a population of slaves, where the sun always illuminates a palace that stays white, where the air is impregnated with perfumes, where birds sing of love, and where you die when you can no longer love...."

"And where you die together!" said Paquita. "But let's not leave tomorrow, let's leave right away, let's bring Christemio with us."

"Pleasure is the most beautiful climax of life. Let's go to Asia, but, child, in order to leave, you need a lot of gold, and to have gold, one has to put one's affairs in order."

She didn't understand any of this.

"There's gold up to there, here!" she said, raising her hand.

"But it's not mine."

"What does that matter?" she said, "if we need it, let's take it."

"It doesn't belong to you."

"Belong!" she repeated. "Haven't you possessed me? When we possess each other, it belongs to us."

He began to laugh.

"Poor innocent! You know nothing of the things of this world."

"No, but here is what I know," she cried out, pulling Henri onto her.

At the very instant when de Marsay was forgetting everything, and was consolidating his desire to appropriate this creature forever, he received at the height of his joy a dagger thrust that went right through his heart, mortified for the first time. Paquita, who had pushed him vigorously above her to contemplate him, cried out, "Oh! Mariquita!"

"Mariquita!" the young man cried out, turning red. "Now I know everything I didn't want to believe was true!"

He leaped to the wardrobe where the long dagger was kept. Fortunately for her and for him, the wardrobe was locked. His rage increased at this obstacle; but he recovered his calmness, went to get his cravat, and came towards her in such a fiercely significant way that, without knowing what crime she was guilty of, Paquita nonetheless understood that her death was in the offing. So she leaped in one single bound to the end of the room to avoid the fatal knot that de Marsay wanted to loop around her neck. There was a fight. On both sides suppleness, agility, vigor were equal. To end the struggle, Paquita threw a cushion between her lover's legs that made him fall; she took advantage of the respite this advantage left her to press down the spring that was attached to a warning bell. The mulatto arrived right away. In the blink of an eye Christemio leaped onto de Marsay, pinned him to the ground, put his foot on his chest, the heel turned towards his throat. De Marsay understood that if he fought he would be instantly crushed at one signal from Paquita.

"Why did you want to kill me, my love?" she asked him.

De Marsay didn't reply.

"How have I displeased you?" she asked him. "Speak, let us explain ourselves."

Henri kept the phlegmatic attitude of the strong man who feels he has been conquered; cold countenance, silent, thoroughly English, which proclaimed his awareness of his dignity through a temporary resignation. Moreover he had already thought, despite his fit of rage, that it wasn't very prudent to endanger his reputation with the law by killing this girl without warning and without having prepared the murder in a way that would guarantee his impunity.

"My beloved," Paquita went on, "speak to me; don't leave me without a loving farewell! I don't want to keep in my heart the terror you've just set there. Why won't you speak?" she said, stamping her foot in anger.

In response de Marsay fixed her with a look that so obviously meant *You will die* that Paquita rushed over to him.

"You want to kill me, then? If my death can make you happy, kill me!"

She made a sign to Christemio, who lifted his foot from on top of the young man and moved away without letting any judgment, good or bad, of Paquita be seen on his face.

"That is a man!" de Marsay said, pointing darkly at the mulatto. "There is no devotion like one that obeys friendship without judging it. You have a true friend in this man."

"I will give him to you if you want," she replied; "he will serve you with the same devotion he has for me if I tell him to."

She waited for a word in reply, and continued in tones full of tenderness: "Adolphe, give me a kind word. It will soon be day."

Henri didn't answer. This young man had one sad quality, for anything that resembles strength is regarded as a great thing, and men tend to deify excess. Henri didn't know how to forgive. Flexibility, which is certainly one of the blessings of the soul, was meaningless to him. The ferocity of the Northmen, with which English blood is quite strongly tainted, had been transmitted to him by his father. He was unwavering in both his good and bad emotions. Paquita's exclamation was all the more horrible for him since he had been dethroned from the sweetest triumph that had ever swollen his male vanity. Hope, love, all emotions had been exalted in him, everything had blazed in his heart and in his intelligence; then these flames, lit to illuminate his life, had been blown out by a cold wind. Paquita, stupefied, in her suffering had only the strength to give the signal for departure.

"This is useless," she said, throwing aside the blindfold. "If he no longer loves me, if he hates me, it is all over."

She waited for a look that didn't come, and fell down, half-dead. The mulatto looked at Henri with such a horrifyingly significant gaze that he made this young man tremble for the first time in his life—a man whom everyone acknowledged had rare courage. "If you don't love her, if you have caused her the slightest suffering, I will kill you." That was the meaning of this swift look. De Marsay was led with almost servile care along a hallway lit by slits in the wall, at the end of which he went out through a secret door to a hidden stairway that led to the garden of the San-Réal mansion. The mulatto made him walk carefully along a lane of linden trees that ended at a little gate opening onto a street that was deserted at that hour. De Marsay made note of everything. The carriage was waiting; this time the mulatto didn't accompany him; and, when Henri put his head out of the door to look again at the garden and the mansion, he encountered the white eyes of Christemio, with whom he exchanged a look. On both sides it was a provocation, a challenge, the announcement of a war of savages, a duel where ordinary rules didn't apply, where treason and perfidy were the methods permitted. Christemio knew that Henri had vowed Paquita's death. Henri knew that Christemio wanted to kill him before he could kill Paquita. Both understood each other wonderfully.

"The adventure is getting interestingly complicated," Henri said to himself.

"Where does Monsieur want to go?" the coachman asked him.

De Marsay had himself driven to Paul de Manerville's house.

For more than a week Henri was absent from his house, without anyone knowing either what he was up to during this time, or where he was living. This withdrawal saved him from the mulatto's fury, and caused the ruin of the poor creature who had placed all her hope in the one she loved as no other creature has loved on this Earth. On the last day of this week, around eleven at night, Henri came in a carriage to the little gate in the garden of the San-Réal mansion. Three men accompanied him. The coachman was obviously one of his friends, for he stood up straight in his seat, like a man who, like an attentive sentinel, was listening for the slightest noise. One of the other three stood outside the gate, in the street; the second stayed standing in the garden, leaning against the wall; the last one, who was holding a bunch of keys, accompanied de Marsay.

"Henri," his companion said to him, "we are betrayed."

"By whom, my good Ferragus?"

"They are not all sleeping," the leader of the Devourers replied: "Someone in the house must not have eaten or drunk. Look at that light."

"We have the map of the house; where is it coming from?"

"I don't need the map to know," Ferragus replied; "it comes from the Marquise's room."

"Ah!" de Marsay cried. "She must have arrived from London today. This woman wants to catch me in my revenge! But, if she has anticipated me, my dear Gratien, we will hand her over to justice."

"Listen, then! The thing is done," Ferragus said to Henri.

The two friends listened, and heard weak cries that would have softened the heart of tigers.

"Your Marquise didn't think the sounds would come out of the chimney," the chief of the Devourers laughed, like a critic delighted at discovering a fault in a fine work.

"We alone, only we can foresee everything," Henri said. "Wait for me, I want to go see what's happening up there, so I can find out how their household quarrels are conducted. Good Lord, I think she's having her cooked over a slow fire."

De Marsay nimbly climbed the staircase he knew and discovered the path to the boudoir. When he had opened the door, he had the involuntary shiver that the sight of bloodshed causes even the most determined man. The spectacle that presented itself to his eyes had for him more than one cause for surprise. The Marquise was a woman: She had calculated her revenge with that perfection of perfidy that is the sign of weak animals. She had hidden her anger to assure herself of the crime before executing it.

"Too late, my beloved!" the dying Paquita said, her pale eyes turned towards de Marsay.

The Girl with the Golden Eyes was expiring drowned in blood. All the lit torches, a delicate perfume that could be smelt, a certain disorder where the eye of a fortunate man would recognize the mad whims common to all passions, showed that the Marquise had expertly questioned the guilty one. This white room, where blood stood out so clearly, betrayed a long struggle. The bloody prints of Paquita's hands stained the cushions. Everywhere she had clung to life, everywhere she had defended herself, and everywhere she had been struck. Whole strips of the cinnamon-colored hangings had been torn out by her bloody hands, which must have struggled for a long time. Paquita must have tried to climb up to the ceiling. Her bare feet had left prints along the back of the divan, on which she had no doubt climbed. Her body, torn to shreds by her executioner's dagger, showed how single-mindedly she had fought for a life that Henri had made so dear to her. She was lying on the ground, and, as she was dying, she had bit the muscles of the instep of Mme de San-Réal, who held in her hand a dagger soaked in blood. The Marquise's hair was torn out; she was covered with bites, many of which were bleeding; and her torn dress showed her half naked, her breasts scratched. She looked sublime. Her greedy, furious head gave off the smell of blood. Her gasping mouth remained half-open, and her nostrils weren't wide enough for her gasps. Certain animals, when enraged, leap on their enemy, kill it, and, calm in their victory, seem to have forgotten everything. There are others who circle around their victim, who guard it, afraid someone might come and take it away, and who, like Homer's Achilles, circle around Troy nine times, dragging their enemy by the feet. That is how the Marquise was. She didn't see Henri. First of all, she was too aware of being alone to fear witnesses; plus, she was too drunk with hot blood, too animated by the struggle, too exalted to see all Paris, if the city had formed a circle around her. She wouldn't have felt lightning. She hadn't even heard Paquita's last sigh, and thought she could still be heard by the dead girl.

"Die without confession!" she said to her; "go to Hell, monster of ingratitude; belong to no one but the devil. For the blood you have given him, you owe me all of yours! Die, die, suffer a thousand deaths, I've been too kind, I just took a little while to kill you, I could have made you suffer all the torments you pressed on me. I will live! I will live unhappy, I am reduced to loving no one but God!" She contemplated her. "She is dead!" she said to herself after a pause, coming violently back to herself. "Dead! Ah! I will die of suffering!"

The Marquise wanted to throw herself on the divan, overwhelmed by a despair that took her voice away, and this movement allowed her to see Henri de Marsay.

"Who are you?" she asked him, running to him with her dagger raised.

Henri stopped her arm, and they could thus contemplate each other face to face. Horrible surprise made frozen blood flow in the veins of both of them, and they trembled on their legs like frightened horses. In fact, two twins couldn't have resembled each other more. They both said the same thing: "Is Lord Dudley your father, then?"

Each of them nodded in the affirmative.

"She was faithful to blood, at least," Henri said, pointing at Paquita.

"She was as free of guilt as possible," Margarita-Euphémia Porrabéril continued, throwing herself on Paquita's body and letting out a cry of despair. "Poor girl! Oh! If only I could bring you back to life! I was wrong, forgive me, Paquita! You are dead, and yet I live! I am the unhappiest woman there is."

At that instant the horrible face of Paquita's mother appeared.

"You're going to tell me you didn't sell her to me so that I could kill her," the Marquise cried out. "I know why you're coming out of your den. I'll pay you for her twice. Be quiet."

And she went to get a bag of gold out of the ebony wardrobe, scornfully throwing it at the feet of this old woman. The sound of gold had the power to outline a smile on the motionless physiognomy of the Georgian woman.

"I've come just in time for you, my sister," Henri said. "The law will ask you...."

"Nothing," the Marquise replied. "One single person knew about this girl. Christemio is dead."

"And this mother," Henri asked, pointing to the old lady, "won't she want a ransom for her?"

"She comes from a country where women aren't human beings, but things with which you do what you want, things that are bought and sold, things that are killed—things used only for your whims, the way you use furniture here. In any case, she has a passion that makes all other passions give in, and that would have annihilated her maternal love, if she had loved her daughter; a passion..."

"Which one?" Henri said impatiently, interrupting his sister.

"Gambling; may God keep you from it!" the Marquise replied.

"But who are you going to get to help you," Henri said, pointing to the Girl with the Golden Eyes, "to remove the traces of this fantasy, so that the law won't prosecute you?"

"I have her mother," the Marquise replied, pointing to the old Georgian woman, to whom she made a sign to stay.

"We will see each other again," Henri said, thinking about his friends' anxiety, and realizing the necessity of leaving.

"No, my brother," she said, " we will never see each other again. I am going back to Spain to enter the convent of Los Dolores."

"You're still too young, too beautiful," Henri said, taking her in his arms and giving her a kiss.

"Farewell," she said, "nothing can console me for losing what seemed to us both the Infinite Being."

Eight days later, Paul de Manerville met de Marsay at the Tuileries, on the terrace of the Feuillants.

"Well then, what's become of our beautiful Girl with the Golden Eyes, you big rascal?"

"She died."

"From what?"

"Her chest."

Paris, March 1834—April 1835